TERROR
AT THE SOO LOCKS

To

Ronald Lewis

October 18, 1996

TERROR
AT THE SOO LOCKS
A NOVEL

Ronald J. Lewis

AGAWA PRESS

MACKINAW CITY, MICHIGAN

Additional copies of this book may be ordered through bookstores or by sending $12.95 plus $3.50 for postage and handling to:

Publishers Distribution Service
6893 Sullivan Road
Grawn, MI 49637
(800) 507-2665

Copyright ©1997 by Ronald J. Lewis
Cover design by Cynthia Shimek
Text design by Mary Jo Zazueta
Library of Congress Catalog Card Number: 96-85424
ISBN: 0-9642436-1-X

Printed in the United States of America

10 9 8 7 6 5 4 3 2 1

To my grandchildren

ACKNOWLEDGMENTS

I would like to thank the following persons for supplying information for *Terror at the Soo Locks*. It was important to me to make sure that every action necessary to the plot was technically possible, and logistically plausible. These are the people, or groups, who verified the accuracy of selected parts of my fictional narrative.

U.S. Coast Guard, Sault Ste. Marie

LCDR   Preston Gibson
LT   Thomas Cafferty
LT   Lillian Maizer
MK1   Steve Koskinen
BM2   Dan Munns, USCGC Buckthorn

U.S. Coast Guard, Cheboygan
U.S. Coast Guard, St. Ignace

Albert G. Ballert, Great Lakes Commission, Ann Arbor
Julie Neph, General Engineer, Mackinac Bridge Authority
Captain John Wellington, Wellington Maritime, Sault Ste. Marie
Fabian & Joanne LaTocha, Mackinaw City
Brian Jaeschke, Sault Ste. Marie

TERROR
AT THE SOO LOCKS

CHAPTER 1

The *Singapore Soo*, a general cargo ocean freighter, measuring 590 feet in length and 75 feet at the beam, left its home port on June 6, 1996. It traveled from Singapore to the Philippines to pick up a load of exquisite mahogany furniture. It was destined for Chicago, and on to the Soo Locks at Sault Ste. Marie, Michigan. One round trip voyage of the *Singapore Soo* was equal to circling the globe.

The ship's owners, Asian Pacific Transport, Ltd. had a long term contract with the Algoma Steel Company in Sault Ste. Marie, Canada to haul specialized steel products, on its return trip, for delivery to manufacturers in Singapore and its neighboring countries. The *Singapore Soo's* name was selected because it was designed and built in 1988, specifically for this contract.

The Captain, Wayne Chung, was born in Singapore when it was still a British Protectorate. In Chinese, his name would be Chung Weng Ho, but when his family became Christians, they began calling him Wayne. In his capacity as a sea captain, he spent so much time with English speaking people, and Western culture, that he found it more expedient to follow their ways.

He was 17 years old when the Japanese Armies swept through Southeast Asia. He was captured in 1941, and sent along with the Allied prisoners, mainly British, to build the Bridge on the River Kwai. He somehow managed to survive the ordeal in which 65,000 Allied soldiers died at the hands of the Japanese.

Captain Chung married a Singapore woman in 1949 and they had one child. Both his wife and child died in the Asian flu epidemic of the 1950s. He spent most of his life on ships, earning the reputation as an excellent seaman. He had worked as a captain for several shippers, and worked for the Asian Pacific Transport Company for the past ten years.

After its month long journey across the Pacific Ocean, through the Panama Canal, and the St. Lawrence Seaway, the *Singapore Soo* arrived in Chicago on Thursday, June 27th, where it discharged its cargo of furniture.

On Friday and Saturday the crew had free time, and spent the evenings experiencing their own style of entertainment in one of their favorite cities. The crewman with the least seniority was normally selected to guard the ship, but Captain Chung volunteered to stand watch so all of the members of the crew would be free to go.

Sunday, June 30, 1996

The *Singapore Soo* resumed its voyage northward, up Lake Michigan, on Sunday morning. By early Monday morning it had eased under the Mackinac Bridge, and through the narrow channel between Mackinac Island and Round Island. It reached the town of Detour at 7:30 a.m.

All ships traveling to and from the Soo Locks must pass through a thirty-five mile section of the St. Mary's River, a channel between the U.S. and Canada that connects Lake Superior and Lake Huron. When the ship entered the St. Mary's River at Detour, the river pilot, Gordon Roberts, climbed up the Jacob's ladder to board, taking over from the lake pilot.

Gordon Roberts was a World War II hero. He was born in the Canadian Sault in 1926. His parents migrated across the border to Sault Ste. Marie, Michigan in the 1930s, where he graduated from high school. After the war he returned home and joined the Coast Guard stationed at the Sault. He became mayor for a few terms, and was liked by almost everyone in town. In his later years he enjoyed working, on call, for the Wilson Maritime Company as a pilot for foreign ships passing through the St. Mary's River and the Soo Locks.

The burly Roberts, entered the bridge of the *Singapore Soo*, taking over the helm from the lake pilot. He would steer the freighter up the St. Mary's channel, and through the Soo Locks.

"Captain Chung, good to see you again. Let's see, your last trip through here was early last November, wasn't it?" Gordon had looked forward to seeing the cheerful Asian seaman.

"And then.... we had that meeting in Singa...."

Gordon stopped abruptly, noting that the lake pilot hadn't quite left the bridge.

"You are quite correct, Mr. Roberts. How could I forget.... it was in November, your month of storms." Captain Chung's reply was typical of his cultural formality, and revealed his Asian accent. He didn't quite say Mr. Loberts, but there was a noticeable ellishness in his Rs.

"As you probably recall, Mr. Roberts, there were thousands of Amelicans (he couldn't quite make it with that word) who came to the Mackinac Bridge that day to welcome us to your country. We Singaporians were so happy to know that the Amelican people admired our strict adherence to the law, in spite of your President's scolding for the spanking of that Amelican boy. Many people waved at us from the bridge that day to show their approval."

"We—lll!" Gordon was reluctant to explain that it was the Labor Day Mackinac Bridge Walk that brought the people there, not the colorful foreign freighter, and that the walkers love to wave at the ships as they sail under the bridge. So he just clammed up.

Captain Chung burst out with an oriental-tinged laugh! "How would you Amelicans say it? I really had you going on that one, didn't I? Now, Mr. Roberts, we both know that it was your Labor Day holiday, the day of the famous Bridge Walk, led by your honorable governor, that attracted thousands of people, not our humble ship!"

The *Singapore Soo* plodded slowly up the St. Mary's River toward Sault Ste. Marie and the Soo Locks. About half-way from Detour to Sault Ste. Marie all ships encounter Neebish Island. At this point the channel is so narrow that upbound ships have to be routed to the east, and downbound ships through a narrow passage, called the Rock Cut, to the west of the island.

Just before reaching the top of Neebish Island a new crewman, named Chaw Wi Chan, approached the First Mate, Kee Lim, "Mr. Lim, how soon do we expect to reach the Soo Locks. I am anxious to see the Poe. I hear that it is even larger than Panama's Gatun Locks."

"Yes, and the American pilot, Gordon Roberts, said that we will probably enter the Poe, instead of the MacArthur. He and Captain Chung just heard from the lockmaster that the *Federal Bergen* will still be in the MacArthur. And there will be no 1,000 foot lake freighters approaching from either direction for several hours. They would take precedence over us.... for the Poe Lock.... that is. So we should enter the Poe at one-thirty.... and be on our way shortly after two o'clock."

Chaw Wi Chan thanked First Mate Lim and walked to the cabin section. He disappeared into the hold of the ship.

Fifteen minutes later, as the *Singapore Soo* moved cautiously up the St. Mary's above Neebish Island, an oriental man, dressed rather neatly for a seaman, climbed surreptitiously down the Jacob's ladder at the side of the Singapore freighter, left there because of the numerous changes in pilots, and swam to the shoreline, apparently unobserved. He disappeared into a wooded obscurity.

Twenty-five minutes later, on its slow trek to the Soo, the *Singapore Soo* passed the downbound *Kapitan Malaga*, a 575 foot general cargo freighter, registered in Hong Kong. As the *Kapitan Malaga* idled through a narrow section of the St. Mary's, Captain Kam Quon turned the helm over to the first mate and walked in his officious manner to the stern of the ship. He slowly lowered a Jacob's ladder to water level, turned around and returned to the helm.

The *Singapore Soo* reached Sault Ste. Marie thirty minutes later. The *Federal Bergen*, a 591 foot ocean freighter, registered in Norway, was in the MacArthur Lock, named for General Douglas MacArthur. Only two locks were in operation, the MacArthur, 800 feet long and 80 feet wide, and the Poe Lock. The Davis was seldom used, and the Sabin was closed permanently.

The Poe, named for a Civil War Colonel, is reputed to be the largest, and probably one of the most active locks in the world. At 1,200 feet long and 110 feet wide, the Poe is the only lock in the entire St. Lawrence Seaway System wide enough for the fourteen 105 foot wide ore carriers in the Great Lakes fleet.

As the *Federal Bergen* was trudging slowly out of the MacArthur Lock, the lower gate to the Poe Lock opened ceremoniously to admit the inconspicuous foreign freighter, the *Singapore Soo*, into its captivity. The mighty Poe appeared much too spacious for its pint-sized visitor.

〰️

Gordon Roberts was at the helm, alone in the bridge with Captain Chung.

"When will you be back in Singapore, Captain Chung? I have orders from George to meet you there as soon as we both can arrange it."

"The *Singapore Soo* will return by way of Honolulu, to Hong Kong, and then to Singapore. We are scheduled to be there by August 7th."

"Will the Singapore Girl meet with us again? That will make my trip more enjoyable. I know she is one of George's.... associates.... like us.... but is she also a personal friend of yours?"

Captain Chung said, "She is our only link for solving...." The captain hesitated, "You understand what I mean. Yes, I have grown fond.... I should say very fond of her. Only as a friend of course. I am old enough to be her father.... and I have a great respect for her."

〰️

Three seconds later, before either man could say another word, at precisely 1:48 on that Monday afternoon of July 1, 1996, the lives of Captain Wayne Chung and Gordon Roberts ended abruptly and violently as multiple explosions split the cabin of the *Singapore Soo* apart. The blasts ruptured the entire rear section of the freighter, and ripped off the lower level gates of the gigantic Poe Lock.

While in the lock, the ship had been lifted about half of the 21 feet from Lake Huron to Lake Superior. When the lower gate was blown open, the water rushed out, flushing the *Singapore Soo* back into the lower harbor, and smashing it against the stern of the *Federal Bergen*.

Before it was flushed out of the Poe Lock, large metal pieces from the side of the *Singapore Soo* had torn into the visitor's tower, which was filled with excited tourists. They had been, just minutes before, thrilled to see the *Federal Bergen*, and were anticipating the entry of another colorful foreign freighter into the locks.

The visitor's tower was on the other side of the MacArthur Lock, but broken glass and debris was seen falling after the particles from the ship struck the side of the tower. Then screams were heard as the tourists saw the body of a woman plunging to the ground from the stairway at the south end of the tower.

Small fires were breaking out all over the ship. The building with the control tower had been closest to the blast. James Harp, the lockmaster in the control tower, was knocked off his chair by the force of the first explosion. He managed to get up and call the Coast Guard Operations Commander Gilbert. The Sault Coast Guard Headquarters was only a few hundred yards downriver.

Commander Gilbert said, "We'll have the *Katmai Bay* out there in fifteen minutes. Thank God it's Monday. The crew's on duty. Then we'll set up a security zone and stop traffic on the St. Mary's. Are you hurt bad, Jim?"

"No.... I just got knocked down.... I'm okay. Try to get John Wilson if you can."

The *Katmai Bay* was stationed right there at the Sault. The 140 foot Icebreaking Tug with two fire monitors, or water cannons, was underway in less than fifteen minutes. One of the Wilson pilot boats was already in action, rescuing sailors who had jumped into the water. The *Katmai Bay* approached the *Singapore Soo*, with its water cannons snuffing out the fires on deck. The *Federal Bergen* had minor damage, and was able to continue southbound out of danger.

Personnel from the Army Corps of Engineers were at the scene in a matter of minutes. Fire engines and police from Sault Ste. Marie and the surrounding area rushed to the scene. Fire fighters from the Canadian Sault drove across International Bridge to help. Chaos ensued for the next several hours.

CHAPTER 2

Three days before the *Singapore Soo* was to leave its home port for its journey to Chicago, and to Sault Ste. Marie, a crew member, Mr. Kwen Ho, was found dead by the Singapore police. He was found in the vicinity of the docks with a broken neck. Captain Chung had assigned the task of replacing him to the first mate, Mr. Kee Lim.

Just two days before sailing, a presumed itinerant seaman, giving the name of Chaw Wi Chan, bumped into the first mate and applied for the job. The Captain was forced to make a quick decision. With no time to properly appraise his credentials, Captain Chung hired him, knowing that Chaw Wi was no ordinary seaman.

Because of the long voyage from Singapore to Sault Ste. Marie, Captain Chung had persuaded the ship owners to allow the general cargo vessel to make a stop at Honolulu. Since the owners considered him their most capable sea captain, they always arranged for a small portion of the cargo, food products, to be destined for the Hawaiian Islands.

They assumed it was for his personal pleasure, or that he was being kind to his crew. Captain Chung knew that it was a treat for the crew members, who looked forward to spending a night or two in Honolulu. But there was another reason that Captain Chung had for stopping in Honolulu, and neither the crew nor the owners would ever know that reason.

At the first sight of the Aloha Tower in Honolulu Harbor the crew always cheered. The crewman with the lowest seniority was required to stay behind to guard the ship. After the Hawaiian cargo was unloaded, Captain Chung, the first mate, Kee Lim, and the other sixteen crew members walked from the docks to Ala Moana Boulevard, in the heart of downtown Honolulu. Some walked the short distance to Chinatown, while a small group always preferred to take a cab to the Pearl City Tavern.

"I'll see you back at the ship in the morning, Kee."

"Yes sir, 10 o'clock Captain." Kee replied.

The captain did not mingle with the crew members. Carrying an overnight bag, he walked straight to Wo Fat's Restaurant, which is in the center of Chinatown. The television series, *Hawaii Five-O*, had made Wo Fat a notorious enemy of Jack Lord, but Captain Chung knew that there never was a person named Wo Fat.... only a restaurant. The restaurant was now closed, and there was no sign of activity anywhere. He had a key for a side door and entered the building.

Inside he was met by a man named George, who said, "Greetings Captain Chung. We have much to talk about. Your usual room is ready."

Captain Chung said, "Thank you, George. I have much to report since my meeting with Hui Ming and Gordon.... and that professor. I don't know how that American professor got mixed up in this. I think he was teaching in Singapore at the time and Gordon happened to know him."

"There's more to it, Captain." It was strange, but no one dared to call Captain Chung by his first name. His dignified manner of speech, and his impeccable appearance were almost intimidating. He presented such a genteel image that he appeared to be authoritative. To the contrary, he was a formal, but kind and thoughtful man.

George continued, "The professor has worked for us in the past. That might be why Gordon invited him."

The captain said, "That may explain it. I was not aware of that. Actually, Gordon did not talk about our current project while the professor was present. It seemed to be just a treat for his scholarly friend to enjoy the company of a Singapore Girl. They are icons, like movie stars, in our country.... as you well know."

George said, "Perhaps Captain.... at that time, Professor Kendall did not know about this project. Now please tell me.... what have you uncovered since our last meeting?"

While Captain Chung and the crew were in Honolulu during the night, the newest crew member, Chaw Wi Chan, had been assigned to guard duty. On this particular trip, at 2:35 a.m., a 30 foot motor launch pulled alongside the *Singapore Soo*, at anchor in the Honolulu harbor. Chaw Wi helped the sole occupant of the launch unload several boxes unto the deck. The two men disappeared into the hold of the freighter, Chaw Wi reappearing on deck at frequent intervals to perform his guard duty. After approximately three hours the launch motored away into the darkness.

In the morning Captain Chung left Wo Fat's and walked to the dock. First Mate, Kee Lim, met him at the dock at 10:00 a.m. sharp. Within minutes every crew member had returned to the ship. Then, at exactly 12 o'clock noon, the *Singapore Soo* resumed its long, slow journey to Chicago, on the other side of the world.

A few days later, Captain Chung was standing on deck, enjoying the peaceful blue waters of the Pacific Ocean. The new crewman, Chaw Wi Chan, walked up to him.

"Captain Chung, I am not so familiar with our journey. As you may recall, we made our arrangements so quickly that I only know that our destination is Chicago. What route do we take to arrive there?"

The captain had already sensed by his looks and manner of speech that this man was not the typical seaman. Chaw Wi used the language of a well educated person, and he always looked neat, unusual for an itinerant seaman.

Captain Chung surmised that he might have become an alcoholic and was searching for an escape. He had observed many such oriental men who tried to adopt Western customs and ended up as alcoholics. He wondered why anyone would drink anything other than his delicious Oolong Tea.

Captain Chung truly believed that alcohol was the way in which the devil entered into men's minds. He had seen many crazed seamen die as this serpent caused them to commit acts of violence. How foolish, he thought.... that the only intelligent animal on earth could betray God by using alcohol and drugs to destroy the gift of reason. But, alas.... the good captain was too wise to let it bother him.

Captain Chung began to explain the route to Chaw Wi, "We are moving at an average speed of about fourteen knots, so we should arrive at Panama on June 17th or 18th. The Panama Canal is 40 miles long, and has six locks. They are all the same size, 1,000 feet long and 110 feet wide. The Atlantic is about 170 feet higher than the Pacific, so the *Singapore Soo* will be raised up 55 feet by the two Miraflores Locks, 31 feet by the Pedro Miguel Lock, and 85 feet by the three Gatun Locks, to the sea level of the Atlantic Ocean."

"We will then turn northward along the East Coast of the United States to the mouth of the St. Lawrence River, 1,000 miles Northeast of Montreal. After we pass Montreal we will enter the first lock of the St. Lawrence Seaway, which is the Canadian, St. Lambert Lock. It will lift us 15 feet from Montreal Harbor to the Laprairie Basin."

"The Seaway has four Canadian locks, and then two

U.S. locks, which lift the ships a total of 226 feet to Lake Ontario. Canadian pilots will begin at the mouth of the St. Lawrence River. They will change at Quebec City, Three Rivers, and again at Montreal."

He continued, "I trust that you know, Mr. Chan, that foreign ships must have pilots who know the waters. Even though I could easily do it, the Canadian and American laws prohibit me from piloting this ship through the entire Seaway system."

Chaw Wi said, "You and I both know that the requirement of pilots is more of a tariff, than it is a safety measure, honorable captain."

Captain Chung realized that he was rambling on.

"Are you becoming bored with all of these numbers, Mr. Chan? I am sorry if I have given you a superfluous geography lesson."

"On the contrary, Captain Chung. I am delighted to hear every detail."

Considering the long tedious trip ahead, Captain Chung was also delighted to continue.

"At the first American lock, the Snell, another pilot will board. From this point into the Seaway, pilots may be either Canadian or American. A new pilot boards at Cape Vincent, near the city of Kingston, for travel into Lake Ontario, and another at Port Weller, to enter the Welland Canal."

"Niagara Falls drops a maximum of 167 feet, but the difference in the sea level of the two lakes, Ontario and Erie, is 326 feet. We take a cumbersome, but amazing, voyage through the 27 mile long Welland Canal. It has seven lift locks, all measuring 766 feet long and 80 feet wide. Each one lifts us an average of 45 feet. Then the eighth lock is a guard lock, that is.... it has no lift.... but it is the longest lock in the world at 1,380 feet. So the seven Welland Canal locks will lift us from the 246 foot sea level of Lake Ontario, to the 572 foot sea level of Lake Erie."

"At Port Colbourne, as we enter Lake Erie, another pilot will board us to guide the ship to Detroit. He will depart at the Detroit River where a mail boat will deliver another pilot, who will guide us past Windsor and Detroit, into Lake Huron. With one more pilot exchange, we will then sail northward toward the Straits of Mackinac, under the majestic Mackinac Bridge, and into Lake Michigan."

Chaw Wi Chan asked, "When do we arrive in Chicago?"

"I expect...." Captain Chung stopped to do some calculating, "to arrive at Chicago on June 27th. That is on a Thursday. You will have some time to enjoy Chicago.... probably two days. Then on June 30th we will resume our journey to the Soo Locks at Sault Ste. Marie. We should arrive there on July 1st. I am looking forward to seeing my friend Gordon Roberts. I have been informed that he will be our pilot through the St. Mary's River and the Locks."

Chaw Wi Chan smiled with an undetectable touch of insolence, and said, "I am sure that you and your friend will have an unforgettable time together."

Captain Chung wondered why Chaw Wi would think that a simple meeting of two friends would be unforgettable. But then, this mysterious man was not an ordinary seaman, and would not be expected to make predictable comments. The good captain would never know that Chaw Wi Chan's statement had been made with deliberate and ominous significance.

CHAPTER 3

T he entire population of Michigan's Upper Peninsula was shocked as the news of the bombing circulated among the towns. Not since 1941, just before the bombing of Pearl Harbor, had there been a presumed threat to the Soo Locks. Military leaders convinced President Roosevelt that Hitler might order Nazi planes to bomb the Soo Locks in order to stop the flow of iron ore to the steel mills in Detroit, Pittsburgh and Gary, Indiana.

The scare resulted in the urgent building of two airfields, one at Raco, 25 miles southwest of Sault Ste. Marie, and one near Kinross, Michigan, 20 miles south of the Sault. Both air strips were built in 90 days. Then, after Pearl Harbor, 20,000 troops along with barrage balloons were sent to guard the Locks. This time the threat was more likely from Japanese Kamikazi bombers. Some residents claim that enemy planes were actually sighted.

After World War II, Kinross became Kincheloe Air Force Base, with a 12,000 foot runway for landing B52 bombers. The Kincheloe Air Force Base was closed in 1977, but the runway is used as a landing field for the Chippewa County International Airport. Air Force One landed there in 1992 when President Bush walked the Mackinac Bridge on Labor Day with the Michigan Governor.

Sam Green, FBI agent stationed in Detroit, flew in a Lear Jet to the Chippewa County Airport, arriving at 4:46 p.m. Reino Asuma, Chief of the Sault Ste. Marie Police Department, met Agent Green at the airport, and drove him directly to the Soo Locks.

WSOO-TV news reporter, Susan Young, met them at the scene, followed by a scraggly dressed cameraman. He scurried after her as she persistently held out the microphone, shoving it into Reino's face. Susan and Reino had grown up together in the Soo. They were in the same grade all through school, and were as close as brother and sister. They were now pushing 40, that age of questioning life's goals.

"Reino, Reino. Is it true that Gordon Roberts was on the ship? Is he dead? And I heard that seven crew members were killed. Come on, Reino, I need to know!"

"Look Sue, I'll let you know as soon as I verify the damage. Now, shut up and get out of the way until I ask Oscar."

Susan just pointed to her microphone and to the cameraman, gave Reino a big grin and said, "That'll sound great when they show this on the 11 o'clock news!"

There were crowds of people milling around, trying to find out what had happened. Reino spotted Oscar in the security office under the sightseeing tower. He and Sam pushed through the crowds.... Reino yelling, "Hey Oscar.... Oscar."

Susan and her cameraman pushed and shoved people out of the way to get in closer, knowing that Reino would eventually allow her to nose in.

Oscar Bobay, the sexagenarian city coroner, dressed in his ancient, frazzled looking black suit, wrinkled blue shirt, and coffee-splashed tie, verified that Gordon Roberts, the Captain, and seven crew members were dead.

He said, "Jim Harp was in the control tower, Reino. He was shaken up a bit.... but not injured. One senior citizen, a female, was thrown from the visitor's tower. She died almost instantly. And several other tourists were injured by flying glass and debris. Lucky for them the MacArthur is the first lock. It looks like the Poe is 150.... maybe 200 feet away from the visitor's tower."

Oscar also added, "The *Singapore Soo* scraped along one side of the lock as it was pushed backward. And Reino.... I heard some guy from the Army Corps of Engineers say it would take at least two weeks to clear all the damage to the side of the lock, and to repair the gate. That lower gate is completely blown apart.... they have to practically build a new one.... he says."

"And get this.... Commander Gilbert of the Coast Guard

told me that if the ship had already been raised the full 21 feet, and the upper gate had been opened.... or blown open, the waters from Lake Superior would have surged down into the level of Huron and swamped the entire harbor."

Susan was listening to every word. "What do you think caused it, Oscar?" She interjected quickly before Reino shoved her back.

"Well it was obviously a bomb, or bombs. Most of the tourists and the workers heard at least three explosions," Oscar offered.

Sam grabbed Oscar's hand and said, "I'm Sam Green, FBI. We'll have an investigating team here within a few hours. The Coast Guard is technically in charge, but due to the high probability of terrorism, either domestic or international, they will cooperate in the investigation with the FBI. Reino here has been cluing me in to the local situation.... I'll appreciate everyone's help in clearing this up as soon as we can."

"Mr. Green, is it okay to call you Sam?" Susan asked without expecting or wanting an answer. Sam Green was an Afro-American, born in Detroit. His family lived on the west side out by Grand River and Wyoming. He was a star football player for Mackenzie High in 1971-72. He maintained his trim, muscular shape over the years. On duty, he normally wore a dark suit with a white shirt, button-down collar, and a conservative tie. It was a hot day, even in the Sault, so he had to be satisfied with a summer-weight cotton suit, and a short-sleeved white shirt.

Susan persisted, "Is this like the Oklahoma City bombing back in April of '95? Do you think it might be another domestic-based terrorist attack? Or do you think it was foreign terrorists?"

"No comment, yet," Sam answered. "Give us a few hours to sort out the facts and get some answers. In fact, you better give us a few days!"

TUESDAY, JULY 2, 1996

The next day, Reino, Sam and Oscar met at the Police Station, in Reino's unpretentious office. Susan tried to squeeze in unnoticed between Sam and Oscar, but Reino was wise to her tactics. With one powerful arm he picked her up and deposited her outside the door.

"You can watch us from out there, Sue," Reino chided.

He really admired Susan's ethical professional standards, but he loved to tease her. Perhaps it was more than just fun. After all, neither one had stayed married. They had both tried, but marriage failed; that common American affliction.

"Well, what do you think Sam?" Reino queried.

"There are four crewmen with minor injuries, and the rest have no injuries, whatsoever. They were up front and just jumped into the water after the ship was flushed into the harbor. Your friend Gordon Roberts, Captain Chung, and the seven crewmen who died, were in the middle of the ship, or below deck. But, according to the first mate, Kee Lim, who survived the blast without a scratch, there should be one more. He says there were eighteen men in the crew, not including Chung. He said a new crewman using the name Chaw Wi Chan was missing from his station for about an hour before the ship entered the locks."

"And get this. He told me that the crewman this guy replaced was found dead in Singapore, just a few days before sailing. Then this guy, Chaw Wi Chan .... boy that name sounds familiar.... bumped into the first mate and Captain Chung at the docks and applied for the job. Chung needed someone desperately, so he hired the guy without having time for the usual paperwork and precautions."

"Go ahead and let the lady in now Reino, if you want to," Sam suggested. "I don't mind telling her.... and the rest of the news reporters.... what we know in general.... but no mention of that guy, Chaw Wi Chan. That name sounds like an alias, doesn't it?" The name amused Sam, but he didn't quite know why.

"Oh, and before I forget. I have Kee Lim held in protective custody so that no one can ask him any more questions. Only the three of us know about Chaw Wi Chan. So let's keep it that way, it's very important!"

Susan barged in when Reino opened the door. She took very little time to ask for the details. "Why was the *Singapore Soo* bombed? We know how, what and where, but not why."

"We don't know who either, Susan," chimed in Oscar, who remained observant, but almost timid, during these sessions. He had an M.D. from Wayne State University and was a good pathologist. But he had spent his entire life in the Upper Peninsula of Michigan, most of it in Sault Ste. Marie. He had never seen a black person until he travelled to Detroit in 1942, when he was twelve years old. He grew up saying "youse guys" until he went to study at Wayne. He was unsophisticated when it came to the question of national and international implications. Too young for World War II, and in college or too old for the other wars, Oscar had no desire to venture into the world outside. It frightened him.

Susan asked, "What about the implications of the bombing? Was it done to kill people? Or was it done to interfere with our steel industry? And how about the cargo. Was the *Singapore Soo* carrying a mysterious cargo?"

"I'll try to partially answer your questions, Miss Young," Reino began, facetiously treating her with formality, but with respect for her as a professional.

"First the cargo. The *Singapore Soo* was empty. It discharged its cargo of Philippine mahogany furniture at Chicago. It was heading for Algoma Steel's docks right here in the Canadian Sault. It would take on a cargo of specialized steel for manufacturers of small electronic products in the Pacific Rim countries, including Malaysia, Indonesia, Thailand, and Singapore."

"Thank you Chief Asuma." Susan paid him back with a little formality of her own.

Reino ignored her dig and went on. "Next, let's consider the international implications. Damaging the Poe Lock will stop all of the 1,000 foot lakers from supplying the U.S. steel industry for a while. Remember there are only 13 of them. But there are other lakers—about 30 of them—that are limited by either beam or draft to the Poe. Like the *Roger Blough*. It's only 850 feet long, but it's too wide for the other locks."

Reino continued, "Let's face it, the overall effect would be negligible. The steel furnaces always stockpile supplies of iron ore for contingencies. And besides, the entire Canadian fleet is built to go through every lock in the St. Lawrence Seaway System. The Algoma Central fleet has 22 ships alone. Almost all of their ships and the rest of the American fleet can go through the MacArthur, the Davis, and the Sabin Locks."

"But the Davis and the Sabin aren't being used right now, are they? Oscar interjected, now in his own territory.

"No, but only because they haven't been needed. For a long time now, they have been talking about combining the Davis and the Sabin into one gigantic lock, even bigger than the Poe. But in the last ten years, or so, the iron ore traffic has gone down, because of foreign competition. The Davis is still operable, and could be used, but not the Sabin, " Reino concluded.

"So," Sam added, "the motive of creating a serious industrial problem for the United States is rather doubtful. In fact, it seems out of the question."

"And as far as killing people, an average of about 120 people die in traffic accidents every single day of the year, and there is no coverage by the national press or TV networks. It is not considered a national catastrophe. But, if one airliner goes down with 120 people, only once a year, it is on the national TV news for at least a week."

"Like airplane crashes, bombings are more spectacular, which makes them newsworthy. But the toll of ten people does not come close to that of the Oklahoma City bombing.

And there.... the bombers deliberately killed a large number of people, including children.... making it an unspeakable crime.... a horror story beyond our worst fears. The press won't react the same to this bombing.... with eight foreigners and two Americans dead."

"Wait a minute," Susan protested. "What do you mean, always blaming the press! We are as sensitive as everyone else. I know I won't get a Pultizer Prize for this story, but it's definitely going to stir up national concern. Another bombing.... on American soil. People dead! The biggest lock in the world! Come on! This is big news! I know you probably don't know who did it.... or you wouldn't tell me anyway. But all I need to know is who might have done it. Please?"

Sam Green wasn't going to let the press or anyone else know about the missing crewman, Chaw Wi Chan.

"Sorry, Miss Young, switching to the formality of his FBI training, but I have no idea who or why, yet! This bombing makes no sense to us until we know more about that ship, the *Singapore Soo*, and its occupants."

Sam Green stopped right there with any official verbal statements. Sam had discovered something that no one else knew about. In his thoughts he said to himself, "I may not know who, or why, but I know just the man who can help."

$$\sim\!\!\sim$$

That night, Stacey and Jed, and Dave and Maureen, the anchors of the two regional television stations, and the national press and television networks reported on the bombing at the Poe Lock.

Jed announced, "According to Sault Ste. Marie's Chief of Police, Reino Asuma, a total of 5,300 ships had passed through the Soo Locks in the previous year, 1995. He said that if all the locks had to be closed for the repair work on the Poe Lock, an estimated 150 to 200 ships could be delayed each week."

The national networks announced that the Singapore Goverment had politely requested that a thorough investigation be made of the bombing. For the next week the bombing was in the headlines. Accusations were made against the organized militia groups around the country, and especially in Michigan. After no possible connection could be found with the militia movement, the news switched to the Middle-East terrorist groups. Nothing, such as the type of bomb, the target, the method used, could link the bombing to any of the logical groups. So the news returned to its regular topics after surpassing the public's attention span, and the bombing became history.

CHAPTER 4

Reino drove Sam to the Chippewa County Airport, where an FBI Lear Jet was waiting. Sam Green was anxious to get back to Lansing. He shoved his right hand out to Reino.

"Thanks, Reino. I appreciate your professionalism, especially since we must keep this thing quiet. It's hard to find people you can trust these days. Right now I have an idea who might be able to shed some light on this weird case. In fact... he could be someone you know. You two are about the same age. He told me that he grew up in Mackinaw City.... and I'm sure he still has a cottage there. His name is Bradley Kendall. He's a professor at Michigan State. In fact.... he and Gordon Roberts were good friends."

"No kidding.... he and I played junior league hockey against each other a few times, Sault Ste. Marie against Mackinaw. We were both lousy players, but we sure had fun. We even got in a fight once.... his poor nose! His mother called me a bully."

Chief of Police Reino Asuma was a brute of a man, six feet tall, and strong enough to throw Paul Bunyan over the Mackinac Bridge..... as a struggling burglar, collared by Reino, once described him. His parents, both born in the Upper Peninsula of Michigan, were pure Finns. After two years taking general requirements at Lake Superior State University he became interested in law enforcement. He finished his bachelor's degree and joined the local police department. He became Chief of Police in 1993.

Sam waved to Reino as he boarded the plane, "I'll keep you informed as soon as I know any more. Thanks again."

≈≈

Sam had left Sault Ste. Marie shortly after noon. He arrived at the Lansing airport at 1:35 p.m. Twenty minutes later he was picked up at the front entrance of the airport by an inconspicuous dark blue sedan. Sam used the car phone and immediately called the College of Business at Michigan State University. Bradley Kendall had just finished his last class for the day. Sam caught him as he was coming in his office.

"Brad, this is Sam, you know Sam Green, your ol' buddy. I just flew back from the Sault."

Bradley spontaneously reacted, "Oh yeah, the bombing of the Poe Lock. For gosh sakes, what happened? The news is so vague about it. It was a Singapore ship, I read. And Gordon Roberts was killed.... that would be a loss to the community. I sure liked him a lot. He was the mayor, when Reino and I played junior league hockey in the Sault. He impressed all of us kids with his kindness."

Sam said, "I know the news about the bombing was confusing, but there has to be a reason behind all this. Right now I need your help. Can you have dinner with me at Kellogg Center, at six sharp?"

It wasn't really a question. Sam sounded too serious for anything but an okay!

Sam arranged for a quiet location for the two men to have, what Brad expected to be, an unimaginative dinner at the university student-run hotel. Far from mundane, the first two items on the menu reminded Brad of Singapore.... Chicken Nantua, crowned with scallops, mushrooms and bay shrimp in a rich lobster sauce, and Oriental Cashew Chicken with stir fried vegetables. And then there was good old Lake Superior Whitefish, sauteed, with roasted red pepper and buerre rouge, which sounded like red butter to Brad. And Grand Traverse Chicken, broiled and accompanied by Michigan fruit relish of blueberry, raspberry, and dried cherry.

"You told me last month that you were going to lecture in Singapore again. Is that true?" Sam began.

"Right, this time I leave on Wednesday, July 10th.... for about two weeks. I'll stop overnight in Honolulu, then through Tokyo, Narita airport, that is, on the way to Singapore. The Pacific Rim Institute has me scheduled for seminars in Kuala Lumpur first, and then a week later in Singapore."

"Good, good.... but how about that group in Honolulu.... are you still working with them?" Sam glistened.

"Well, I'm not involved with any specific assignment right now.... if that's what you mean," Bradley offered. "But they know that I'm still on their team if they need me."

"Great, great," Sam leaned forward with obvious enthusiasm. "I need you, and we need them."

Sam explained every detail about the bombing including the missing seaman, Chaw Wi Chan. Bradley burst out laughing at the name.

"It's obviously an alias, a name made up by someone, probably an Asian, who has been watching old Charlie Chan movies, but go on."

"You get the picture, Brad? I need you to contact the Honolulu group you work with. Now, I'm going to level with you."

"What do you mean? Haven't you been all along? I would hope!" Brad bristled.

"Oh sure, but I left one small item out, until I was sure that you'd help. This is something I didn't even tell Reino or Oscar. When I checked the *Singapore Soo* over.... most of the cabins were above the water level.... I found this piece of paper in this guy Chan's cabinet drawer. Here.... take a look at it. Your name's on it.... only it's backwards."

Brad looked at the wrinkled piece of paper. It had four

names written on it. The names were Chung Weng Ho, Roberts Gordon, Lee Hui Ming, and Kendall Bradley.

Brad said, "They're all backwards, like mine and Gordon's. Captain Chung's Chinese name must have been Weng Ho."

"Now do you see why I wanted you to help me?" Sam exclaimed.

Brad was startled, "I sure do. Chung and Roberts are dead and my name is with theirs.

"Who is this Ming guy? I thought you might shed some light on his name."

"No, sorry, it sounds like so many Chinese names. Sounds like a girl's name.... and it's probably written backwards too."

"Brad, didn't you lecture at the same seminar in Singapore last year? Did anything unusual happen?"

"I gave the same seminar in both Kuala Lumpur and Singapore last year. I don't remember any problems; everything went smoothly .... as I recall."

"You know Brad, the note with the four names was on stationary from a hotel in Kuala Lumpur.... the Melia. Is that name familiar?"

"Oh I didn't see that. It sure is. The Pacific Rim Institute.... that's the group that runs the seminars.... they put me up in the Melia during last year's seminar. It's a Spanish-owned international hotel chain."

"Oh, wait a minute.... I.... "

Brad wasn't sure why, but he instinctively stopped himself. He remembered that last year Gordon Roberts called him at the Melia Hotel in Kuala Lumpur and invited him to lunch. Brad was delighted to see the affable old friend. Gordon brought two other people, a Captain Chung, and an absolutely stunning Singapore Airlines stewardess. He couldn't be sure of the name, or of anything for that matter, immediately after seeing her for the first time.

But her name could well have been Hui Ming. He had heard that they are called Singapore Girls. He was so enthralled with her classic beauty, her exquisite manners, and her humility, that he couldn't eat much. But by that time (he had already been in Kuala Lumpur for five days), the only thing he could stomach was bread pudding. The food was much too spicy for Brad, but the Melia Hotel had the best bread pudding in the world. After the third day in the hotel, the waiters automatically brought him the bread pudding.

The meeting seemed to have no substance, just chatting, while Brad sneaked frequent peeks at the scrumptious Singapore fringe benefit (the Singapore Girl, that is.... not the bread pudding). That is why he couldn't see any significance in the lunch meeting. So he decided to just keep it to himself until, and if, it became significant. That Singapore Girl could have been Hui Ming Lee. That means that the four people, whose names were on the note, were at that lunch. And that two of them are dead.

He deliberately withheld this information from Sam. It seemed to have nothing to do with the bombing of the *Singapore Soo*. The two men killed, Captain Wayne Chung and Gordon Roberts, just happened to be on the ship at the same time. No one would blow up a ship in the Soo Locks just to kill two men. It doesn't make any sense.

≋

Brad immediately rescheduled his flight to allow two extra days in Honolulu, and called his friend, Billy Chin at his home on Waimanalo Beach, next to Kailua, on the Windward side of Oahu.

"Hi Billy, I'll be in Honolulu on Monday, July 8th, two days earlier than I had originally planned, so I'll have time to see you. I'll just stay right at the Airport Holiday Inn. United flight 3 arrives at 5:45 p.m., which will be.... let's see.... about midnight in Lansing time, so I'll be too sleepy to enjoy your.... your.... effervescent company," Brad searched for the right word.

Billy was indeed good company, humble but confident; modest but sophisticated. He was a Detective Columbo behind a facade of gullibility. He had received a Ph.D. in Biology at the University of Hawaii at Manoa, and was currently working on an agricultural research grant obtained by the University. He also worked as a part-time real estate agent during lean times between grants.

"Can you meet me tomorrow for lunch or dinner? It's pretty important. I'll rent a car at the airport and drive out to Waimanalo.... and then.... where ever you say."

"Don't be silly, Brad. I'll pick you up at the luggage area. You will stay at my place, I insist! And then tomorrow we can go to either Kailua or Kaneohe for breakfast."

Brad knew that Billy wouldn't have it any other way so he just capitulated. They were schoolmates for a few years back in East Lansing in the late 1960s. Bradley's family lived in Mackinaw City when he was born in December of 1959. In 1964 the family moved to Spartan Village, the married housing units at Michigan State University, where his father was studying for his Ph.D. in Civil Engineering. The two families lived next door and became good friends. Bradley and Billy both started kindergarden at the Spartan Village grade school.

Three years later Billy's family moved back to their home in Waimanalo on Oahu. Bradley's father became a Professor of Engineering at the University of Michigan. In 1968, his family bought a 100 foot waterfront lot in Mackinaw City, on the Straits of Mackinac just west of, and in full view of the Mackinac Bridge. They had a small, but convenient log cottage with three bedrooms, built on the lot in 1970. Bradley, with his mother and sister, spent most of the summers at the cottage in Mackinaw City while his dad taught Summer School in Ann Arbor. They needed the extra money to afford both homes. They were not wealthy, but they always seemed to have plenty.

After finishing high school, Brad attended Northern Michigan University in Marquette. He received his bachelor's degree in Accounting in 1982. He passed the CPA exam on the first attempt, and worked for Page, Olson & Company, a local accounting firm in Mt. Pleasant. Two years later he finished an MBA at Central Michigan University. Then in 1992, he finished his Ph.D. at the University of Michigan, and became a full-time faculty member at Michigan State University in East Lansing, with a joint appointment in Accounting and Finance.

At CMU, his favorite professor was Dr. Roy Nelson, who was now a visiting professor at the University of Hawaii at Manoa. The Nelsons had a cottage along the Straits in Mackinaw City near the Kendall's family cottage. Brad's father and Professor Nelson were good friends. Dr. Nelson had recommended Brad for the courses in Hawaii, and also gave his name to Balbir Singh, Director of the Pacific Rim Institute in Singapore.

CHAPTER 5

MONDAY, JULY 8, 1996

B rad flew from Lansing to Chicago in a United Express 19-passenger commuter. He hated them with a passion because you couldn't stand up; you had to bend over to walk to your seat. From Chicago he flew directly, in a roomy DC10, to Hawaii, arriving at the Honolulu International Airport at about 6:00 p.m., only 15 minutes after the scheduled arrival.

For the first-time tourists, that initial glimpse of the Hawaiian Islands is like going to heaven, a tropical lush green heaven. They can feel and smell it in the air, a warm spiritual tingling that transforms them into a new person.

The best explanation of how Hawaii affects the first-time visitor came from Brad's friend and mentor, Professor

Roy Nelson. It was 1984, the first time that Dr. Nelson taught an extension course for Central Michigan University at a military base on Oahu. On their first Sunday, he and his wife, Eleanor, found the Waikiki Baptist Church, near the intersection of Kuhio and Kalakaua Streets, an ideal location for tourists. During the service an older Hawaiian tutu in a colorful muumuu stepped forward out of the choir. She was the perfect reflection of what every tourist had seen in pictures of lovely Hawaiian dancers.

The organist began to play the Lord's Prayer. As the choir softly sang the words to the Lord's Prayer, she danced the slow Hawaiian hula, where the hand and arm movements tell a story. Spontaneously, and at exactly the same moment, both Roy and Eleanor burst into tears. It was embarrassing, but they sobbed uncontrollably, with joy, until the end of the dance. It was truly a spiritual prelude to Heaven.

Brad, although this was not his first trip to Hawaii, always received that same feeling just before landing at Honolulu International Airport, when the pilot banked the plane in a turn and announced, "As we prepare for the landing, if you will look out the right side of the cabin, you will get a good view of Diamondhead"

The view of the inside of the crater from the air is far different from the side view the tourists see from Waikiki Beach. Excitement surged into his veins at the realization of finally arriving in Hawaii!

"Hi Billy!" Brad was glad to see his old friend. He wanted to give him a big hug. But he had an intuitive sense that

Billy's cultural respect for formality didn't include the man to man hug.

"Aloha Brad!" Billy knew that Brad didn't go for the traditional tourist treatment, leis and all that Ah..low'..ha stuff. Brad considered himself a Kama'aina, practically a native; certainly not a tourist. Although he was a Michigan State professor, Brad had taught for the Central Michigan University Extension Program, once at Kaneohe Marine Base, and once at Hickam Air Force Base. He just loved Oahu, Honolulu, the other islands, and even Waikiki. Best of all he loved the international, primarily Asian, mixture of people.

By the time the two men tossed the luggage in the trunk of the 1990 Mercedes 190E it was seven o'clock, already dark in Honolulu. In Sault Ste. Marie it would be broad daylight for two more hours at 7:00 p.m. But of course, it was really 1:00 a.m. EDT in Michigan, and Brad was staying awake on excitement alone.

"Do you know what this car would cost new in Singapore, Billy?" asked Brad with an air of.... I know something you don't know. He pulled this often with Billy because he knew that he was a walking encyclopedia.

"Well I suppose in Singapore dollars it would be 50 to 60 thousand," Billy guessed.

"More like 120, in Singapore dollars, Billy, which is between 70 and 80 thousand US dollars, depending on the exchange rate." Brad seemed proud of his knowing something that Billy, of Chinese and a mixture of Hawaiian ancestry, didn't know about a predominantly Chinese country.

"And get this, the registration fee each year for an automobile is about 12,000 in US dollars," Brad proudly announced. "In Michigan we pay $100 or so for registration, and we still gripe."

"That's you mainlanders, always griping about something," Billy couldn't help getting in a dig.

Instead of driving on the expressway, Billy drove down Nimitz Highway, which would take them through downtown Honolulu and Waikiki. He knew his old friend would love it, tired or not.

"There's where the old Central Michigan University office used to be," Brad pointed to the two-story office building.

When Brad taught in Hawaii, in 1990 and 1991, he had reported to the CMU Office, which was halfway between the airport and downtown Honolulu. A year or two later, after the downsizing of the military, the enrollments in the graduate programs in Hawaii dropped. The new, smaller office had been moved to Kailua, on the Windward side.

They drove through downtown, past the Aloha Tower, and onto Ala Moana Boulevard headed for Waikiki. They turned onto Kalakaua Street and passed the Hilton Hawaiian Village, said to be the only remaining American-owned waterfront hotel in Waikiki. The colorful lighted streets were busy with tourists enjoying the warm air.

"What's happening with Fort DeRussy?" Brad asked, recalling that Fort DeRussy was used in World War II, the Korean War, and the Viet Nam War, as a rest and recreational hotel for veterans.

"Well, I guess it's still operating as usual, as an R & R

for the military. More like a vacation spot now, with no wars going on."

"Isn't it ironic that the bases, like Pearl Harbor, and the other military properties, like DeRussy, are about the only ocean front properties not owned by the Japanese. They wouldn't have bombed us if they could have seen the future!" Billy mused.

They stopped at the light in front of the Royal Hawaiian hotel and shopping center.

"Can you imagine, the Moana, the Halekulani, and the Royal Hawaiian. These are historical gems.... they were standing during the attack.... and now all foreign-owned. It's a good thing that the government holds on to some good ocean front property or it would all be gone."

"But don't blame the Japanese," Billy reminded his good friend. "They followed the rules of the game. It was the sellers who were greedy."

"I agree," Brad acceded. "They have done a lot to modernize the old hotels. Look at the Moana...it was becoming a dilapidated mess before the Japanese owners remodeled it."

The Mercedes chugged along the world famous Waikiki beach. He turned left on Kapahulu Street next to the Honolulu Zoo and Kapiolani Park. A few minutes later Brad spotted the famous bakery on Kapahulu Street.

"Have you had any Malasadas lately, Billy?"

"No, I was waiting for you to visit again. Last time we both gulped down six Malasadas before we made it back to Waimanalo. I'll bet I gained ten pounds when you were here."

"Well I'll be just as bad this time. I just have to go to King's for breakfast, the Royal Hawaiian for the buffet, the Willows for dinner.... and then to the Ward Warehouse, or is it the Ward Centre.... to the Yum Yum Tree, Horatio's, and Stuart Anderson's."

Brad was exaggerating, of course, but he really meant it.... if he had more time.

Billy moaned, "Sorry ol' pal, but the Willows and King's Bakery are gone. King's set up a bakery in California that ships those delicious Portuguese sweet rolls all over the mainland. And Horatio's has a new name with a similar menu, but not the same."

Brad said, "And I thought I was mad when they closed the Canlis Restaurant. These are.... I should say were.... some of my favorite restaurants. Remember how on Thursday lunch at the Willows, Irmgard Ilulu and her daughters entertained.... and sometimes the locals.... wahines and kanes both.... would just get up and dance whenever they felt like it."

"Well, don't worry," Billy comforted him, "I have a couple of new places to take you tomorrow night. Would you mind if Alina comes with us?"

"Are you kidding.... you know I just adore your sister," Brad smiled. He last saw Alina when she was eight years old. He had a little crush on the big sister, who was only a year older than the two boys, but at that age seemed like an adult to Brad.

The Mercedes turned onto Waialae Avenue and merged into H1 on the way to Hawaii Kai. They passed Kahala where the famous Kahala Hilton, favorite hotel of all the celebrities, was being remodeled and renamed. Another loss of Hawaiian tradition. At Hawaii Kai, Dolly Parton's restaurant, the Dockside Plantation, a favorite of Billy's, had changed ownership. But that was several years ago, before Brad taught on Oahu.

They wheeled along Kalanianaole Highway. Brad had to practice pronouncing that over and over again, but still fumbled it. Just like Kapiolani and Kamehameha. One day in his class at Hickam Air Force Base he mentioned King Kamehameha.

He apparently massacred the pronunciation. One of his helpful military students told him how to pronounce it after class. And a radio announcer clued him in on how to pronounce Kapiolani. But he always stumbled over Kalanianaole.

During the daylight hours, the drive from Koko Crater to Waimanalo was one of the most beautiful drives in the world. Even at night it was a delight. The Underwater State Park at Hanauma Bay, the Halona Blow Hole, Sandy Beach, and Sea Life Park were favorites of the tourists. Brad loved the turn at Makapuu Point, where you could see all the way from Rabbit Island to Kailua Bay, with the lush Koolau Mountains in the background.

But he was almost too tired to notice this time; he dozed off a few times as Billy hummed away, happy to see his old buddy again. They arrived at Billy's humble, but a gold mine measured in market value, house on Waimanalo Beach. Brad just loved Billy's place, but he was dead on his feet.

Billy plopped him into bed at 8:15 p.m., and called his sister, Alina.

"Hi Alina, this is Billy. Brad is here.... he just fell asleep. He'll probably wake up at six in the morning so I'm going to go to bed a little earlier tonight. Otherwise I'll be half asleep when he wants to talk. Let's have lunch at the Koa House in Kaneohe. Brad will love their fried Mahi- Mahi. See you there at.... let's say about 11:30. That'll be about dinner time for Brad so he'll be hungry."

"Fine with me Billy, you know, I'm actually a little anxious to see Brad.... but I don't know why. It must be that if you like him he has to be okay," rationalized Alina.

Alina Chin, now 37, had turned out to be a striking caucasian-oriental mixture of beauty. She looked purebred Hawaiian and loved to dance the hula, but only occasionally on weekends for the free Kodak show. She didn't want to be a professional tourist attraction. She had long flowing black hair, and a petite figure abundant with those things that attracted men's gazes. But she had those two important attributes, missing in so many of the young mainland women, humility and altruism.

Alina had majored in Hospitality Management at the University of Hawaii, graduating in 1980. Brad stayed with Billy during the two five-week periods that he was teaching at the military bases, but Alina was then working in San Francisco. So they hadn't seen each other since they were kids. She was now the Customer Relations Manager at the historic Halekulani Hotel.

CHAPTER 6

TUESDAY, JULY 9, 1996

The next morning Brad woke up at eight. He looked out at the enormous expanse of Waimanalo Beach. A six mile stretch of sand and blue-green water with white- capped six foot waves rolling endlessly into the shore. But best of all it was touristless. The swimming tourists loved Waikiki, the surfing tourists loved Sandy Beach, and the pro surfers loved the monster waves at Sunny Beach. But nobody except the locals and the Kama'ainas went to Waimanalo Beach. The tourists never seemed to wander beyond the main tourist attractions of Waikiki, the Polynesian Cultural Center, Sea World, Hanauma Bay, and the rest.

Some of the houses along Waimanalo Beach were small mansions, but most were just modest tropical homes. Every 80 foot lot on the ocean was worth a million or more. The town of Waimanalo is strictly Hawaiian, undiscovered by tourists. Next to Waimanalo is Bellow's Air Force Base, no longer fully operating, and public beach parks on either side of the town.

Billy's place was unbelievable. The main room was 40 feet long, mostly windows front and back, with a panoramic view of the ocean from Rabbit Island to Kailua Beach. The house, more like a spacious cottage, was completely surrounded by fences and tropical plants, so that only someone inside the locked fence could see inside. It had a convenient kitchen, small bathroom, and two bedrooms. The only shower room was outside, with an extra bathroom for the convenience of swimmers.

Billy said, "Boy did you sleep; it's about two in the afternoon back in Michigan. How about some coffee? But I don't want you to eat too much, because we are going to meet Alina for an early lunch."

Brad's built-in time system always adjusted quickly to time zones.

"Great, you know me; I don't just want coffee, I need coffee." Brad said, making his hands tremble for emphasis.

After a swim in the comfortable ocean water and a little horsing around, the two went back into the house and had some toast and more coffee.

〜〜
〜〜

At 11:15 the two friends hopped in the 190E and drove toward Kaneohe. After passing the Yum Yum Tree Restaurant and spotting a few ducklings begging for food from some children, they drove along Kaneohe Bay Drive. It was a beautiful sight along the Bay, and a nostalgic drive for Brad. They passed the entrance to Kaneohe Marine Base - Hawaii, home of the Red-footed Booby Colony, and where Brad had taught a few years earlier. Billy pulled in and parked in the skimpy lot at the Koa House in downtown Kaneohe.

"The Koa House is more of a breakfast and lunch place. Did you ever eat here, Brad?"

"No, I always went to the Pagoda for breakfast."

Alina had already found a booth. She stood up when they arrived. In Brad's eyes, she was a bundle of petite glamour, 5' 2", and not to sound trite, cute as a bug's ear!

"Alina, I can't believe it. You're grown up... a woman. I expected to see a little girl. I really did."

It may be strange, but he did still have the image of the little girl in his mind. He was pleased to see that her emergence into womanhood had been so successful. Or perhaps, not to be so prudish, her physical development and beauty were impossible for a man not to notice. Alina picked a hand-made lei from her seat and placed it over Brad's head. She kissed him on both cheeks in the traditional Hawaiian custom.

"Aloha, Brad. And you were just a little boy; remember.... I was a whole year older than you two guys. How handso.... that is.... how nice you look."

Alina was not one to flatter, but Brad had turned out to be a handsome young man in her eyes. She liked him instantly.

"Thanks for the welcome, Alina. This is going to be fun, being with you two again."

It wasn't going to be all fun, but they didn't know it yet. This would be the beginning of an experience that all three would never forget.

Billy said, "Brad, try the fried Mahi-Mahi. It's unique here. I'm going to have the pancake sandwich with bacon. And I'm sure Alina will have her typical figure-saving salad, or whatever." Alina scowled at her brother.

~~

After a breakfast they all enjoyed, Alina drove off to the Halekulani Hotel in her 1984 Dodge pickup truck, a favorite of the locals, and Billy drove Brad across the Pali Highway toward downtown Honolulu.

"George wants to see you, Brad."

"What? How did you know about George?"

"Alina and I both joined the Information Network System, we call it the INS, last year. We want to keep Hawaii free from the type of crime that's sweeping the mainland. So we work closely with George. But I never heard just how you got involved with the INS."

"Well it's great to know that you and Alina are on the team, but it can be dangerous, you know. As far as my involvement, my Professor at CMU, Dr. Roy Nelson, asked me to help out when I lectured in Singapore last year. George needed someone incognito, and I guess I fit the bill."

Billy parked in Chinatown, near the old Wo Fat's Restaurant building. Wo Fat's, no longer open as a restaurant, was the center of the intrigue. Wo Fat's was the meeting place for the Information Network System.

George Tong was the brains behind the INS. He had developed a communications system that was capable of tracing criminal activities anywhere in the world. Because it is on an isolated island, Honolulu is unique from all other American cities. The Information Network System was used to monitor the movement of international criminals into Hawaii, particularly into Honolulu. The main concern, of course, was drug traffic, but the system was capable of exposing all forms of illicit activities.

Information is funnelled to George who distributes it wherever necessary. INS never does anything illegal, and merely transmits the information to the police when the situation calls for action. The group has an unofficial approval from the prosecutor's office.

"Professor Kendall, good to see you again. I am very sorry to hear about your friend Gordon Roberts. He worked for us.... as you know.... or did you?"

Brad said, "Not exactly. Gordon invited me to a luncheon last year in Singapore with this Captain Chung, who was killed too.... and now I assume that it was this Hui Ming, who was the Singapore Girl. But they didn't say a word about working for the INS. It turned out to be just a pleasant luncheon for me."

George said, "I apologize for not explaining everything to you last year. We needed someone in Singapore rather quickly, and you were recommended by Dr. Nelson at the

University of Hawaii. Gordon Roberts had my orders to include you with their team on a special mission."

"But then, at the luncheon meeting, Gordon detected that the team was being spied on by someone he recognized at a nearby table. He tried to protect you from being involved with anything suspicious. So he tried to make it look as if you were there merely to enjoy the company of a Singapore Girl."

Brad replied, "I always wondered about that. I couldn't figure it out."

George was a typical Kama'aina Hawaiian, if there is such a thing. They are a duke's mixture of Euro-Asian-Polynesian blood; each with a primary ancestry. George was primarily Chinese. He was casually dressed, as is almost a necessity in the tropics; but he was also neatly dressed, which now seems to be only customary with the older generations. And George's abundant gray hair was evidence that he might be in his fifties.

"Now I'll explain our system to you. This is the most sophisticated information network in the world. We have cooperation from every country in the Pacific Rim, except Cambodia and Viet Nam. Recently even Japan is cooperating, but their organized crime element, the yakuza, is our biggest problem. They are well organized.

We also have cooperation from England, France, Italy, the Netherlands and all of the Scandinavian countries. The local and state police and the FBI cooperate informally by feeding us information as long as we don't get into enforcement."

George continued, "We analyze the movements of all illicit arrivals and departures into the Islands. Our computer system will isolate any abnormal patterns of the American, European, Chinese, or Japanese mafia. These were the major groups. Now it's the terrorists who are bombing buildings, planes and buses. We also monitor numerous groups of drug and arms peddlers. Every ship, from a cooperating country, that enters any Hawaiian port has at least one of our observers on board. The police cooperate so that every plane that lands is scrutinized for shady characters. They pass the raw data to us because our analytical capabilities are superior to theirs. We in turn identify the known members of international underworld organizations."

"You see," Billy interjected, "the INS is the only effective worldwide crime deterrent. George tells me that no known undesirable character can avoid our surveillance. They can't move a muscle without the INS knowing about it. We never use violence or break any laws, but we have been known to physically escort known hit men to the airport, and onto the plane."

~~~

Brad said, "Billy tells me that you wanted to see me, George."

Brad knew that this would not be just a friendly request. He knew that it meant an assignment, maybe a dangerous one. Brad was not a risk taker. He didn't climb mountains, jump out of planes, race cars, or volunteer for anything macho. But he did believe that the INS was the subtle, and effective answer to some of the nation's, and the world's, most serious problems.

"I understand that you are flying to Singapore and Malaysia in a day or two.... is that right?" George knew every detail of Brad's voyage, but his unobtrusive Asian culture prevailed.

"Are you staying at the Melia Hotel in Kuala Lumpur, and the Carleton in Singapore as you did last year?" George did it again.

"Why.... yes. I have to be in Kuala Lumpur on Friday.... let's see that's July 12th. You sure have a good memory, George!"

"I...." George decided not to remind them of his omniscience when it came to itineraries. The INS was geared to trace the whereabouts of anyone. He knew exactly where and when Brad was traveling.... even the last minute change in Brad's plans.

"Well.... I have another job for you to perform. It is not dangerous, in fact you will probably like it." George smiled.

"I would welcome a chance to help, George."

"Good.... when do you arrive in Singapore?" George knew, but had to ask.

"I'll be at the Carleton Hotel on Thursday night, very late, about midnight. Then I fly to Kuala Lumpur early on Friday. I'll only have a little time to shake the jet lag before my Friday seminar. It's from six to ten at night. On Saturday I have from nine to noon, and from one to five in the afternoon. Then I repeat the same format back at the Carleton in Singapore the next Friday and Saturday. I expect to leave Singapore for Honolulu on Monday... let's see...that should be July 22nd."

Brad reached into his safari jacket pocket. He loved to wear his summer weight, beige safari jacket when he traveled because it had so many pockets.

"Yep, here's my ticket. It says that I leave at 7:10 a.m. on July 22nd. But, how come I arrive in Honolulu at 6:50 a.m. on July 22nd? Oh forget it! It's that crazy international date line. It's one day earlier when you travel east."

George just smiled, fully aware of time changes. "I have arranged for you to have lunch on Monday, that will be...." He stopped to look at his notes, "On July 15th."

"I said you would like the assignment because the lunch will be with the Singapore Airlines stewardess named Hui Ming Lee. She will meet you, either for lunch or for dinner at the Melia Hotel. She will tell you exactly what to do."

Brad knew for sure now that this Hui Ming Lee, the name on the piece of paper, was the Singapore Girl he met last year. He wanted to ask more questions, but he knew not to be presumptuous in dealing with George. He provided you with the information, and only the information that you needed to function. And he always seemed to answer the questions you had in your thoughts. But this time he left Brad with some unanswered questions.

George added with an air of finality, "You know now that the luncheon meeting you had at the Melia Hotel in

Kuala Lumpur last year was not a coincidence. You will find out the reason for all that has happened when you meet Hui Ming."

Brad assumed that George knew about the note with the names of Gordon, Captain Chung, himself, and none other than Hui Ming Lee. He seemed to know everything. Or did he? Did George know about Chaw Wi Chan? Probably! The INS knew about surreptitious characters, especially those of Chan's type, one who obviously carried out the plan to blow up the Poe Lock.

George seemed to know every detail about Brad's trip to Singapore, the hotels, and even the times of arrival, so when he didn't offer any more information, Brad didn't ask any more questions. Billy purposely stayed in the background, as if by an understanding. They departed at 4:00 p.m. from Wo Fat's in Chinatown, and drove over the Like Like Highway, through the tunnel under the Koolau Mountains, into Kaneohe and Kailua.

When Brad taught at the Kaneohe Marine Base he found out that Like Like was pronounced licky-licky, and that wiki-wiki, pronounced wicky-wicky, meant fast or quickly. And he knew that the tutus were the pure blood Hawaiian elderly ladies, mostly grandmothers, who taught the children the old Hawaiian customs and traditions. So Brad's favorite quip was, "the tu-tu's wore their mu-mu's as they went wicky-wicky over the licky-licky." Corny, but Brad loved the sound of it.

As they were approaching the house on Waimanalo Beach, Billy curiously said, "Would you mind getting stuck with Alina for dinner. I have to attend a U of H meeting in downtown Honolulu tonight."

Brad knew Billy well enough to guess that he wanted Brad and Alina to have an evening alone.

"Of course, spending an evening with a gorgeous girl is a real sacrifice....but I'll do it for old times sake, Billy boy!"

At 6:30 Alina arrived in her Dodge truck, and brother Billy disappeared.

"I think you've been railroaded," Alina smiled at Brad. "Brother Billy has tricked you into taking me out, I'm afraid."

Brad just smiled. His objectivity in assessing some aspects of the opposite sex was exceptional. He was gifted with an intuitive vision that bypassed epidermic beauty. He was able to perceive the artificial insincerity of those aggressive women who used their seductive beauty to manipulate gullible men. This ploy was used on Brad, a single, attractive college professor, many times by enticing female students. He made sure that his office door was always open; and he would never socialize with a female student enrolled in his class.

He was more attracted to the innate feminine qualities of women, kindness and altruism, that so many of the younger American women have rejected. He liked the Asian-Hawaiian women because so many have retained those feminine characteristics that sensitive and caring men want. These are the men who make good husbands and fathers. They love their children and adore their wives.

For some reason, many young American women try to act like men. But, they imitate their negative qualities, crude language, binge drinking, and promiscuity, instead of their positive ones. These are the qualities of the greedy and egotistical men, and they don't make good husbands. Perhaps this is the reason that so many marriages are failing. Or at least that's how Brad had it all figured out.

"Let's go to Assaggio's, Alina. Billy told me it's your favorite restaurant here in Kailua."

"He's right. They have good salads and the best pasta.... not just good.... gourmet. And they have the best tiramisu in the world."

Brad had never eaten at Assaggio's before. It turned out to be an elegant experience. He selected Fettucini Alfredo. There were more daring selections on the menu, but he was a coward when it came to experimental cuisine. He discovered that the tiramisu was a delicious, moist, custardy, cake-like desert. Since Brad was a cheapskate, as most accounting professors are supposed to be, the reasonable bill was almost as pleasant an experience as the dinner.

Alina's outward beauty was captivating, but her most alluring beauty exuded from within. Brad tried to ignore it, but Alina's charm was beginning to penetrate his almost fearful resistance to women. There was no sinister psychological reason for Brad's sense of inferiority in the presence of women. It was subtle and subconscience.

During a physical exam, his blood pressure taken by a female nurse, was at least ten points higher than when it was taken by the male doctor. The only explanation he had was that, when he was a child, his father's Victorian English-Canadian aunts, both prudish and humble, were so kind to him that he virtually worshipped them. He developed an almost spiritual admiration for women, but not aggressive women.

"That's a pretty dress, ...I mean muumuu!" Brad bravely ventured into foreign territory. He was clumsy at offering compliments to women. He knew it was a muumuu, an exquisite one at that.

"It really is pretty. I like you in that color.... whatever it is, with those.... " He stumbled.

"It's just pink with white flowers." Alina was amused.

Brad was noticing her as a woman. In spite of her humility, she had to acknowledge that she was enticing to men. Too many men had reminded her of it, and tried to take advantage of her innocent friendliness. Several years ago, one of Billy's newly acquired friends drank too much and attempted to rape her. Billy came back from the errand his friend had sent him on, just in time, to throw him out. Alina became aware that she not only had a magnetic personality, but an alluring body as well.

"You know.... I didn't even ask Billy if you were.... well.... you know what I mean.... ?"

"No Brad.... I don't know what you mean."

"Well, you're not married are you?"

"No!" She wouldn't budge an inch.

"Well, are you..... do you have someone like a.... you know.... a boyfriend?" He finally blurted it out.

"No!" She was going to make him work for every bit of information.

"Why?" Brad was honestly bewildered.

"Why aren't you married? And why don't you have a girlfriend? That is of course.... if you don't?" She retaliated, raising her voice just enough to turn a few heads.

Brad looked around and squirmed. "I don't. I guess I am just waiting for someone like.... well.... like you, for instance."

"You don't really know me, Brad. I was just a girl when you last saw me."

"I know, but I do want to get to know you better. Is that all right with you?" Brad searched for her feelings.

"Of course it is. I enjoy being with you, Brad."

During the rest of the evening their conversation centered safely around what they remembered as kids in Michigan. They were both afraid to become serious about their budding relationship. After dinner Alina drove them back to Billy's cottage on Waimanalo Beach.

"I'm sorry you had to be chauffeured around in this old truck."

"Don't be silly, Alina. You and Billy saved me from having to rent a car. But I did wonder why you needed a truck?" Brad searched for a polite way to hide his real feelings about the old clunker.

"When Billy bought his Mercedes he gave his truck to me to use, until I can save enough money to buy a more.... appropriate car. I would never have wanted an old truck, but I couldn't hurt his feelings."

When they arrived at the Waimanalo house, Billy greeted them at the roadside so that Alina wouldn't have to park in his narrow drive. Space was at a premium along the ocean, so there was no room to turn around in many of the drives. Cars had to back out. Brad and Alina both got out of the truck. Alina moved toward Brad to give him the traditional kiss on each cheek.

When he gave her the reciprocal, but noncommittal, platonic hug she relaxed her body in order to, ever so gently.... and ever so deliberately.... press against his. An ecstatic pulsation overpowered him, rendering him momentarily helpless. He wasn't used to this feeling. He usually kept women at arm's length, but these Hawaiian customs made that more difficult.

Alina accomplished her mission to assess his tractability as a mere man at the mercy of a seductive woman. She sensed that moment of weakness that he displayed as her soft body touched his. She had seldom met a man who was such a challenge for her charms. For the first time in her life she had that special feeling of affection throughout her whole being.

She knew that aggressiveness wouldn't work on Brad, so she calmly and stoicly said, "I probably won't see you before you leave for Singapore, Brad. Are you going to stop for a while on the way back?"

Brad knew now that he would definitely stop. If for nothing more than to see Alina. But he wasn't ready to admit it, yet.

"Yes, I should stop to see George on the return trip. And I would like to see both of you again. Is that all right Billy?"

"You bet, my friend! You have a room any time you want." Billy was tickled that Brad was going to stop again. Brad hadn't said anything about stopping on the return trip to see George before this. So Billy could easily guess the real reason for Brad's willingness.

CHAPTER 7

The United Airlines flight, on a Boeing 747, to Tokyo's Narita Airport departed at 11:00 a.m. on Wednesday, July 10. The change in time was quite confusing to Brad. He checked his tickets to figure out why he would arrive in Singapore at 10:10 p.m. on Thursday, July 11.

He figured that it would take about eight hours to fly from Honolulu to Narita Airport. The time difference would be five hours earlier. But when the plane passed over the International Date Line, it would be one day later. So leaving at 11:00 a.m., it would be 1:55 p.m. on Thursday when Brad would arrive at Narita. An almost four hour layover in Narita, a seven hour flight, and a time difference of one hour earlier, would then explain his scheduled 10:10 Thursday night arrival time in Singapore.

For his first seminar in Singapore his flight went to

Hong Kong, so this was Brad's first stopover at Narita Airport. Knowing that Tokyo is the largest city in the world and that Japan is rapidly becoming the world's wealthiest nation, Brad fully expected that Narita Airport would be one of the world's most modern. Upon landing at Narita, the more than 300 people deplaned from the Boeing 747 unto the ground. Brad noticed that there were five automated loading-unloading passenger chutes available, but none was being used for deplaning.

The passengers were squeezed onto buses and funneled through a single customs line. They then went up a one-lane escalator to the main level of the international section of the airport. This gate served the transferring passengers from all international airlines, including United, American, TWA, Air France, British Airways, China Airlines, Japan Air Lines, Singapore Air Lines, Quantas, and Lufthansa.

About 1,000 people were crowded into the main circular waiting area. There was one snack bar with no tables. Upstairs was the first class waiting area, smaller in size and less crowded. There were no prohibitive signs so Brad walked up the stairway. There was one stairway to the first class area on the fourth level, or you could take the only elevator in the entire international area, which held four normal-sized persons with carry-on luggage, or six skinny persons with no luggage.

Brad spent most of the three hours in the first class area, which had a gift shop and a snack bar. You could buy a glass of Coca-Cola for US $3.00, or a bowl of watery soup for US $5.00. There were six tables, each the size of a large serving tray, for a total capacity of twelve people who could sit while eating. Imagine O'Hare or JFK, both airports in cities smaller than Tokyo, with a total capacity for sit-down eating of only twelve people.

There was a door which led to a closed area for those who had special privileges, President's Club, etc. The bell on the outside didn't seem to work so most of them just opened the door and walked in. The carpeting was ripped under the door and was held together by a piece of black tape. The carpeting in the entire first class waiting area was stained and worn.

Four stewardesses from American Airlines were lying on rows of seats by the stairway trying to get some sleep between flights. There was no private area for flight attendants. They had to compete for a place to lie down and rest with the others.

"Don't you have accommodations to rest between flights?" Brad asked.

"This is it! We have to alternate sleeping and watching our luggage." The stewardess yawned a reply. "There's no place to sleep, and they don't even provide a special place to sit down. We have to sit with the passengers."

Brad's flight left Narita ten minutes late; this time through the loading chute directly into the 747. Brad rested, but could never sleep soundly on a plane. Shortly before arriving the passengers had to fill out a form for immigration. It was boldly printed that in Singapore the penalty for drug trafficking is death.

The Boeing 747 landed at Changi Airport in Singapore

right on time. Brad was sleepy, but managed to stay reasonably alert. He loved Singapore. The Changi International Airport was one of the cleanest and most beautiful airports in the world. What a contrast after Narita. Every operation at the airport was efficiently carried out. There were tropical plants decorating some of the waiting areas, and there was even a play area for children. Of course it was empty this late at night.

The immigration officials were polite, but not friendly. They were solemn and perfunctory in their examination of the passport and other documents. If the documents were in order the officials made no comment. No small talk; not even a hello, thank you, or goodbye. Brad attributed it to a cultural difference between the Asians and the garrulous Americans.

Last year, when he had first landed at Changi, he looked for a luggage cart. An immaculately dressed airport attendant immediately brought one to him. Of course, Brad searched for the money slot, taking out all the quarters he could muster. The attendant explained that the carts were free. He tried to tip him, but the attendant politely declined.

He was also surprised that all taxis charged the same fare, $15.00 in Singapore currency. That would be just slightly more than $10.00 in U.S. currency, and no tip was expected. Conversion to U.S. dollars was duck soup for an accounting professor like Brad. Just multiply Singapore (S) dollars by 70%, and Malaysian dollars, called Ringgit Malaysian, (RM) by 50%. The exact exchange would vary a little, but those percentages were close enough in round figures.

The taxi driver was Muslim, Brad surmised by his name, Mohammed. He spoke English, but with the Arab or Muslim accent. The Indians in Singapore had a different version of English, Brad called it the sing-song twang. The Chinese spoke with only a slight Asian accent.

All of the delegates to Brad's Activity-Based Costing Seminar, whether from Singapore, Malaysia, Thailand, or Indonesia, were highly educated and had no perceivable accent. Attendants to the seminar were accounting and financial analysts or managers of large international companies, such as Johnson & Johnson, Texas Instruments, Northern Telecom, Siemens and Royal Dutch Shell. Respectfully, they were called delegates, not students. Their dignified English had none of the slang that has crept into our American version of the English language. Even our American major networks news reporters, are beginning to use crass words like cops, bucks, and you guys. They routinely mispronounce sauna, nuclear, academician, and Massachusetts.

What surprised Brad the most on his first trip to Singapore was that his seminar delegates spoke American, not British, English. After all, the modern version of Singapore was developed by Sir Stamford Raffles in 1819, and the British were influential until 1959, well over a century. He soon learned from the delegates that they had attended American universities.

"Your destination, Sir?" Mohammed asked.

"The Carleton Hotel. Do you know where it is?"

"Yes sir, it is on Bras Basah Road, overlooking the Raffles Hotel. We will be there in about 35 minutes. There is little traffic at this time."

They traveled on the picturesque East Coast Parkway from the airport to downtown Singapore. Upon arriving at the Carleton, Brad became aware of the difference between Honolulu and Singapore, which was only one degree north of the equator.

The hot, humid, night air of Singapore, has almost no variation. There are no seasonal changes. The average summer high temperature is 87 degrees and the average winter high is 84 degrees, with lows in the 70s. Not much variation to get excited about. In Michigan it may change 30 degrees in one day. And Hawaii has breezes that make the tropical temperatures comfortable most of the year.

Brad paid Mohammed and thanked him.

"Here is my card. When you want to take a tour of the city, I will drive you. I give a flat fee, cheap...compared to the big tours. Give me call, please." Mohammed gave his pitch.

"Sure, when I have time, I'll call. Thanks again, Mohammed." Brad knew the system. The taxi drivers received a percentage of the money that the tourists spent at certain shops.

Brad's reservation at the Carleton, made by Balbir Singh, Director of the Pacific Rim Institute, was in order and he checked in promptly, dead tired. He awakened from a sound sleep at 9:00 on Friday morning, looked around the elegantly decorated hotel room, and realized that he was half way around the world from good old Michigan. It gave him a strange, but exciting and challenging feeling to be in Asia.

The phone rang. "Hello Bradley, this is Balbir. How was your flight?"

"Good morning, Balbir. Great. Right on time. I stopped over for a couple of days in Hawaii to see old friends. And other than the usual jet lag, I'm rarin' to go."

"I will drive you to the airport. Let's see, your plane leaves at twelve noon. It is only 250 miles to KL and I see that you will arrive at 12:55."

Balbir, his secretary that is, had made all of the arrangements for the seminar from the point of arrival in Singapore. Most of his lecturers came from Canada, Australia, Britain, or the United States. So the itinerary was similar, except that the length of the seminars varied. Instead of the usual two-day seminar, this time Brad would lecture for four hours on Friday, and all day on Saturday. He would fly into Singapore, spend one night at the Carleton to recover from the jet lag, then fly to Kuala Lumpur the next day. He would have only three to four hours to eat and rest before the seminar began at six o'clock. He had to have superb organizational skills to be prepared for these seminars. Compared to undergraduates and even graduate students, these delegates were the most experienced and advanced audience he had ever lectured to. If he forgot anything in his preparation he couldn't run down to his office and retrieve it.

Brad checked out of the Carleton and Balbir picked him up promptly at 10:30 a.m. As soon as he saw the turban he remembered that Balbir was a Sikh. After last year's seminar Brad's curiosity led him to the library. He read that the Sikhs, from Northern India, were Hindus who believed in one God, and rejected idolatry and the caste system. The source didn't explain why they wore the huge turban, however!

Balbir's conversations with Brad, and probably all of the Pacific Rim Institute's guest lecturers, were well organized and formal.

"The seminar in Kuala Lumpur will be tonight and Saturday. You said that you would like to remain in KL until Tuesday. So I have arranged for you to fly back to Singapore on Wednesday so that you will have two days to relax.... and tour the city if you wish. The Seminar in Singapore will then start on Friday, July 19th at the same time."

"Sounds perfect. I want to see more of both Kuala Lumpur and Singapore this time."

"If you wish, Poh Lay Han will meet you at the airport. Otherwise she will meet you for dinner at the Orchid Room on the lobby floor of the Melia Hotel at 5:00 p.m. She will deliver the program to you with all of the details, your outline, with the time of each segment, lunch break at noon.... and.... whatever else you want to know."

"Is Poh Lay Han someone new. It was Lily Khoo last year. And she doesn't have to meet me at the airport. I know how to get around this time."

"Yes, Lily Khoo left for another job. Poh Lay is our new Administrator for the Kuala Lumpur program. I told her to take care of your every need."

Brad did not assign any special significance to that statement, but he should have.

CHAPTER 8

B albir dropped him off at the airport, and Brad, ticket in order, found his way to the Singapore International Airlines (SIA) gate.

Before he boarded the 727, he watched in amazement as four SIA stewardesses entered the gate. The famous Singapore Girl, who had been selected for Madame Tussaud's waxwork museum in London to represent superior in-flight service. Each pencil thin Singapore Girl wore a full-length exquisite blue-print, Mandarin style dress. Her round face resembled that of a painted oriental doll. Jet black hair and sharply defined eyebrows over the slightly slanted sparkling dark-brown eyes. Crystal clear unblemished skin surrounding bright red lips. Unreal! The synchronization of their every movement could be imitated only by an ambulatory mannequin.

Brad had read in *The Singapore Straits Times* last year about the serious problem with male passengers on Singapore Airline flights. It was reported that Asian men have gone mad with lust, and have attempted to grab and seduce a Singapore Girl during the flight.

And Brad was supposed to have lunch with one on Monday. Heaven forbid! The last time he had lunch with this Hui Ming Lee he couldn't remember any of the conversation with Gordon Roberts and that Captain Chung fellow. Now they are both dead. They might have said something important, but he was mesmerized by Hui Ming's enticing beauty. Not this time, he promised himself!

Brad boarded the SIA flight to Kuala Lumpur. During the flight he filled out the required custom entrance forms, on which, similar to that for Singapore, was printed, "The penalty for drug trafficking is death, according to Malaysian law." The stewardess was indeed very polite and attentive. He was tempted to ask about Hui Ming, but had second thoughts about bringing any attention to her. George did say that she was involved in his mission. That would definitely be a secret, and revealing her identity could be dangerous for her.

♒

Brad's flight landed at Subang International Airport at 12:50 p.m., five minutes early. He proceeded to the immigration clearance. He had filled out a form on the plane that requested the reason for the trip to Malaysia. The choices included tourist and business, but not education. So he had checked the business category.

The immigration officer stopped him and asked if a sponsor was going to meet him. Brad explained his educational mission, to present a seminar, and that his sponsor did not plan to meet him. At the mention of a seminar the customs officer refused to stamp his passport and called in his superior. They both said that he could not enter without a sponsor.

Brad showed them the promotional brochure that had the topic, the dates, his picture and qualifications, and a complete description of the sponsoring agency, the Pacific Rim Institute. The Kuala Lumpur office was listed with the name of the seminar administrator, Poh Lay Han, and the telephone number. Brad gave them Poh Lay Han's office number, but she was apparently out to lunch.

The supervisor finally gave him a temporary admission, but he had to report to the main immigration office in downtown Kuala Lumpur on Saturday morning, the morning of the all day seminar. The immigration office closed at noon on Saturday. He wouldn't be allowed to leave the country until he reported.

Brad argued that reporting to immigration would take away time from the seminar, and that it would penalize their own Malaysian citizens who paid US $1,000, which is equal to RM $2,500. The two customs officers gave no credence to his arguments and continued to require his compliance.

Brad knew enough not to rent a car in either Kuala Lumpur or Singapore. Driving on the wrong side of the street was enough reason. But there were taxis, bicycles, motorbikes, and rickshaws by the hundreds. It was suicide for the unfamiliar. He summoned a taxi and directed the Malaysian driver to take him to the Melia Hotel on Jalan Imbi. Since just about every street began with Jln., for Jalan, Brad assumed that it meant street or avenue. The Malaysian taxi driver's accent was far more picturesque and consequently difficult to understand. The driver knew exactly where the Melia, one of the more expensive hotels in Kuala Lumpur, was. Brad was in no mood for chit-chat, but the driver customarily chatted away indifferent to the passenger's lack of comprehension.

At 2:30 Brad was finally settled in his room, 1206. He flopped into the bed and just relaxed for the next hour. Poh Lay Han was staying in the next room, 1208. She waited until five o'clock before knocking on the door connecting their rooms. Brad was doing some last minute shuffling of notes and transparencies.

"Dr. Kendall, Sir? I am Poh Lay Han, the Seminar Administrator."

"Yes, I'm Bradley Kendall. Balbir told me that you would take care of everything for me. It's good to meet you, Miss Han."

Another shock for poor Brad. Poh Lay was not only gorgeous, but voluptuous, too. Couldn't they find some plain Janes in Asia? He was here for business, strictly business. Well, of course, the culture too. To see the Malaysian countryside and its people. But not to be tempted by all these females.

The pair descended to the Orchid Room on the Lobby floor. It was a typical Malaysian Buffet. Brad shuddered. Spicy entrees. Malay food is full of flavor, with ginger root, lemon grass, tumeric, lime, shrimp paste, chillis, and garlic. A spirited waiter spotted Poh Lay and recognized Brad from the last seminar.

"Good day, Miss Han, and Professor, it is a pleasure to see you again. Do you still like bread pudding?"

Brad looked at his name tag and laughed. "Thank you, Tak. I remember now.... you were the one who took such good care of me last year. I sure do want some of that delicious bread pudding. But I intend to try some of your Malaysian dishes first. Then, when my mouth catches on fire, I'll switch back to the bread pudding again."

Tak began his oft-repeated spiel, "Today's buffet has Malaysia's favorite dish, Satay. The Orchid Room's version consists of barbecued slices of beef, with ketupat, threaded on a skewer, and served with a spicy peanut sauce. It also includes rice wrapped in palm fronds. The Indian section features Marsala, which has curried chicken and a real delicacy, curried fish heads."

"Yuk!" Brad muttered under his breath.

"We have one Beijing dish, featuring braised lamb, with wheat-based noodles. The Hokkien dish, has a variety of shellfish, garnished with seaweed; and the Hunan food is air-cured ham in honey sauce, served with a glutinous rice. Those are the main entrees. Miss Han can probably tell you what all the other items are."

Tak was a slender Malaysian, probably with some Indian blood. Brad could tell by his accent. Both the Malaysian and the Singaporean hotel waiters were unbelievably polite and attentive. Strange, when you consider that they couldn't, and wouldn't, accept tips. Two or three waiters were at your table in a split second if your water glass was low, or if you just turned your head.

"There it is, Sir." Tak pointed to one of the round buffet tables. There it was.... the bread pudding!

Brad and Poh Lay were seated at a corner table with maximum privacy. Brad had to motion the ever attentive Tak aside, so that he could pull her chair out himself and watch Poh Lay delicately sit down. It was fun for Brad. Some of his avant-garde dates would hurry to sit down before he made it to their chair. He loved to wait on women. He adored their purely feminine attributes; their softness, and their tenderness. He wanted to believe that girls were made of sugar and spice and everything nice.

With the buffet they didn't need to look at the menu, so Poh Lay spoke in her dainty little voice. "I have program with me, Dr. Kendall. Would you like see it now or after dining?"

"Let's eat....I mean dine...first." Brad hesitated a second. "Would you be more at ease calling me Brad? I'm not much older than you. And it's perfectly all right with me."

"Please excuse me, Dr. Kendall, but I would rather not."

"I understand Poh Lay....Oh, I'm sorry....may I call you Poh Lay, or do you prefer Miss Han?"

"No! No! You please call me Poh Lay."

Well, that was settled. You never know, thought Brad.

He sampled several of the entrees, excluding the curried fish heads, of course. He found that he was gradually acquiring more tolerance for the less spicy selections, and even discovered that one entree, the Hunan honey-cured ham, wasn't spicy hot at all. As usual, he couldn't resist the warm bread pudding with a creamy custard sauce, to put out the fire in his tongue after tasting some of the other, more typical, buffet specialties.

~~~

The seminar began promptly at six o'clock. There were 12 delegates from Malaysian joint ventures, or subsidiaries, of German, British, Canadian, and American firms. All of the delegates were Malaysian citizens. They were highly qualified accounting professionals. He was amazed that, in a predominantly Moslem country, five of the twelve delegates were women. One of the Moslem women wore her full gown and head covering with only her eyes showing.

Brad began by saying, slowly and enunciating each word carefully, "I was warned to speak slowly so that everyone could understand my brand of English."

That brought some murmuring and a few chuckles. A female delegate, a finance manager for Shell Oil Company in Malaysia, spoke up for the group in a typical mid-American accent.

"Dr. Kendall, you were misinformed. Everyone here will understand you if you speak naturally. Just as you would in one of your classes on the campus in Michigan."

She was right. Everyone in the seminar understood and spoke English perfectly, although some had a distinct British/Malaysian accent. He explained the problem that he had with the Malaysian immigration officials at the airport.

The Malaysian delegates could not explain the behavior of the immigration officials, which only increased the uncertainty of their intent in Brad's mind. They emphasized that the Immigration Headquarters Building closes at noon on Saturday. And there are long lines of people. They warned Brad that it might take all morning just to reach the window. The delegates were quite upset over the circumstances, which would unquestionably interfere with the seminar.

At the eight o'clock break, Brad asked Poh Lay to call Balbir at his house. She handed the phone to him.

"Sorry to bother you this late, Balbir. Did Poh Lay tell you what happened at the airport?"

"Yes. I don't understand why. They have never done that to any other guest lecturer. Another American is giving a seminar on training procedures in Jakarta right now. He gave his seminar in KL last week, and had no trouble at all. In fact he wants another seminar as soon as possible."

Brad said, "They seemed to pick me out for some reason."

"There is one possible explanation." Balbir offered. "One month ago a popular Malaysian official was detained in Boston, suspected of drug trafficking. It turned out that he was innocent. The Malaysians were furious and might have selected you to harass merely because you are an American."

"Well, we can't do anything about it now. I have to report at the Immigration Headquarters Building tomorrow. Poh Lay agreed to go with me, reluctantly."

Brad stopped momentarily to see where she was. He saw her talking to one of the delegates. "She seemed afraid, Balbir. Do you know why?"

"She just moved to KL from Bangkok. She is probably not used to living in a predominantly Moslem country, yet. But, if there is one place she knows well, it is the Immigration Headquarters Building. She will guide you there."

"What about losing time on the seminar?"

"If they complain, we'll refund a portion of the fee. Don't worry, my friend. I'll take care of everything."

CHAPTER 9

B rad and Poh Lay agreed to meet in the lobby at 6:30 on Saturday morning. The doorman hailed a taxi for them. It was still dark at seven when the taxi dropped them off at a narrow lane that lead to the Immigration Headquarters Building. Poh Lay pointed to a dilapidated, four story building at the end of the dark lane, in what appeared to be a dreary section of downtown Kuala Lumpur.

As they walked toward the building, several men from both sides of the street rushed out at them. They were furiously waving their arms and shouting in a foreign language. Brad was frightened to death, but Poh Lay appeared calm. Poh Lay shouted, as loudly as she could with her dainty voice, in Chinese Mandarin, and they quickly disappeared back into the bushes and shadows.

"For gosh sakes, Poh Lay, what did they want?"

"They help fill out immigration forms. Most of people do not understand Malay or English, so.... need interpreter. They charge fee, of course."

Poh Lay read the directional signs on the ground floor. Then the two of them climbed the cluttered staircase to the fourth floor. They waited in the first row of seats for an hour, looking out of place in their business attire. There were people from all over Asia in their native dress. By eight o'clock the room had become an international melting pot. Behind the windows Moslem women in full native dress were scurrying around handing out papers to the clerks at the windows.

Poh Lay told Brad where to line up and he was first in line. No one came to the window until 8:15 a.m. The gruff, expressionless, Malaysian man shuffled papers for another ten minutes. Then he did not speak, but motioned Brad to hand him his passport. He then handed him a form, returned the passport, and motioned for the next person to step up. Not one word.

Poh Lay knew what to do. She quickly filled out the form, went to the front of the line and handed it, with Brad's passport, to the same man. They sat in the crowded room until 9:30. Brad began to feel uneasy. He was sitting there without a passport. If, for some reason they were out to get him, they could just throw him in jail for not having a passport. And he couldn't do a thing about it.

All of a sudden, Poh Lay jumped up and said that they called Brad's name. They had called Mr. Bradley, not Mr. Kendall, and it went right over his head, last names first. The man who had called his name was a higher official and he commenced to bawl Brad out again for some ambiguous reason. Brad explained that Poh Lay was the sponsor's representative, and that she was right here with him. The official coldly approved Brad's passport, but limited his stay in Malaysia to one week. At that point Brad didn't need or want any more time in Malaysia.

When they returned to the Melia Hotel, Poh Lay called the delegates and the seminar was resumed at 10:30, losing only 90 minutes. The seminar, ending at five o'clock, was a reasonable success, considering the circumstances.

After the friendly goodbyes and the usual clearing up process, Poh Lay said that she would take care of all further details. Brad was happy to have a chance to rest before dinner. Poh Lay suggested that they go to the Le Coq d'Or Restaurant on Jalan Ampang, where they obviously serve something other than the spicy Malayan food. On the way to his room Brad picked up a *Kuala Lumpur Straits Times* newspaper at the desk in the lobby. He happened to notice his horoscope. It read:

"Today brings a fighting chance to lift the curtain on a tense and challenging period of hard earned progress and achievement. Your passport to prosperity could get stamped today." He had to laugh out loud at that bit of irony.

At 7:00 p.m. Poh Lay knocked on the connecting door between their two rooms. Brad was ready and they descended to the lobby floor. The doorman hailed a taxi and off they went to the French restaurant. Brad was in seventh heaven with the gourmet French cuisine. He frivolously ordered escargot for an appetizer. Poh Lay suggested that he might like the house specialty, pan fried venison. Then she ordered a goose liver salad. His journey into aristocratic heaven ended abruptly when he received the check. The check totaled RM $140. Brad shuddered as he made his quick conversion to US$70. He used his handy American Express card. The Pacific Rim Institute paid for all his food at the hotel, but when he ventured out on his own he had to pay himself. He tried not to display his cheapskate attitude in front of Poh Lay.

They returned to the Melia Hotel at 10:15, and stopped at the Piano Bar. It was at one end of the lobby, and open to anyone who wanted to sit and listen. The tables were empty except for two Japanese couples. One man was noticeably drunk. Brad had never seen a drunken Japanese businessman before. The woman, presumably his wife, and the other couple, were noticeably embarrassed by his obnoxious behavior. His group managed to drag him off, sensing that he was disturbing the entertainers.

Then Poh Lay said, "That young man.... over at bar. He keep looking at you, Dr. Kendall. Do you recognize him?"

"No, he doesn't look familiar. He probably doesn't see many Americans here in Kuala Lumpur. There are more Australians and Europeans.... and very few Americans."

Poh Lay politely said, "How can he tell difference, Professor Kendall?"

Brad saw the cue for his style of humor, "Aren't we Americans supposed to be ugly?"

Poh Lay took everything the authoritative professor offered seriously, and replied, "Oh no! Professor Kendall; that is not true. I think you are...." She stopped to look closely at him. "Yes.... you are.... ver handsome man."

A Malaysian man and woman, in their late forties, were the entertainers. The woman sang while the man played the piano. They were singing the good old Sinatra, Perry Como, type tunes. When they did "I Left My Heart in San Francisco," Brad asked them to throw in a line or two of, I Left My Heart in Mackinaw City. He hurried up to his room brought his video camera down, and taped it to play to his friends back in Michigan. After a few more songs, he and Poh Lay headed for their rooms. The Kuala Lumpur seminar was over, so Poh Lay's responsibility had ended.

"I'll see you to your door, Poh Lay."

"Thank you, Professor Kendall." She slipped inside.

Fifteen minutes later there was a knock on their connecting door. Brad opened the door and there stood Poh Lay in a black negligee. She had on high heels, and black stockings with a garter belt. Even the word voluptuous was an understatement. Brad was stunned. He gawked for a full 30 seconds, before stumbling for just the right words.

"Come on in, Poh Lay. Sit down right here." Brad wanted her to sit down fast, because his resistance was diminishing quickly when she stood full view in front of him. She was petite all right, but not in all places. Her face and body, enthroned in that particular combination of clothing, were the epitome of a virile man's sexual fantasy. He went to his closet and brought out his summer weight robe and said, "Why don't you put this on while we talk. It will be more comfortable." He meant more comfortable for him, not her.

"Now, why did you come here ready for.....well, you know what I mean."

"I was told by Mr. Singh to take care all your needs. I thought he meant to.... to do this. I work in nightclub in Bangkok before I come here. I had to please the customers whenever the owner asked me. And to keep my job the owner wanted me to please him many times."

"Poh Lay, you are a sweet, wholesome young lady. You work for Balbir, now. He doesn't expect you to give sex to please his lecturers. He wants you to run the seminars, just like you did for me. You were great. Everything went smoothly. You even saved my neck with the immigration."

"But that other American, last week. He was happy to have me.... do.... what I do.... for him. He stay an extra night so I could.... please him more. He want to come back for another seminar.... right away, soon. But Balbir told him it would take six to eight weeks to make all arrangements for another seminar."

Even though appalled by the implications, Brad couldn't help chuckle over the poor fellow's dilemma.

"And I much rather please you. I like you very much. It is more than like. I have special feeling inside for you. Not for that other.... American fellow."

"Poh Lay, I like you too. But not in that way. Pleasing

me with sex doesn't show our feelings. I enjoy you as a person."

"But.... I watch American movies. Man and woman meet in bar. After few drinks they go to apartment or hotel room. Lady rip off man's shirt first. She more aggressive. Then he tear clothes off her, while she slobber all over his face. They jump in bed. Is not what you like, too?"

"No, definitely not.... Poh Lay. Those movies are made by sick people. The producers are money hungry. It's what we call pandering. They go as far as they can, knowing that they will make more money. Unsophisticated people are attracted to sleaze. Intelligent people are not."

"Today's writer's and producers have no imagination, so they just show the same sex scene, over and over, in every movie. And they don't have a good command of the English language, so they use foul language instead."

Poh Lay tried to look understanding, but she did not really comprehend all of Brad's mini-lecture. Like the Americans depicted in the movies, she had been accustomed to using sex as an economic tool, not as a sacred gift of God. She still wanted to capture his heart in the only way she knew how. She threw off the robe and stood up, exposing her scanty attire once again.

All of Brad's philosophical piety went down the drain for the moment, during which her alluring, seductive, and tantalizing femininity captured his attention. He enjoyed it for a full 30 seconds, paralyzed by temptation, before Poh Lay spoke. "Can I dance for you? Like I do in the nightclub in Bangkok. Don't you want to see me dance?"

"Poh Lay, yes.... you can dance for me.... if you.... if you put on that pretty skirt and blouse you wore Friday. I can't explain it, but I don't just want you to.... I really need you to wear something over that.... "

Poh Lay danced provocatively even with her skirt and blouse on. But, the extra clothes were just enough for Brad to survive another episode of the unexpected onslaught of temptation he had been subjected to on this trip. After complimenting her dancing he eased her into a comfortable position on the couch, and pulled a chair over to sit near her.

"Maybe I'm different from other men, Poh Lay, but I have to be in love enough to marry a girl before sex can enter in. I haven't found that one girl, yet. I'd better hurry, I'm already 36."

Poh Lay spoke softly. "I would like to be your girl. But I understand. Our worlds too far apart. You not like men I meet in Bangkok. You like my father. He is good to my mother. I will look for man like him."

"Now, I know you understand, Poh Lay. You do not have to entertain the lecturers. They will appreciate you as a professional woman.... and that's enough. You did a good job."

Brad gave Poh Lay a big hug, and a kiss on each cheek, Hawaiian style. She opened the connecting door, turned around and said, "Thank you, Professor Kendall. I will never forget what you teach me tonight"

Brad couldn't resist, "Well that's what professors are supposed to do..... right?"

Sunday, July 14, 1996

Brad had arranged to take the afternoon country tour of Kuala Lumpur, leaving from the Malaysia Tourist Information Complex on Jalan Ampang, at 2:30 p.m. The spectacular complex of buildings was originally a private mansion called Tuanku Abdul Rahman Hall. The British used it as Army Headquarters in 1941, just before the Japanese invaded Malaya. It became the headquarters of the Japanese Imperial Army during their occupation.

The country tour began with the extravagant white palace, Istana Negara, official residence of His Majesty the King. The tour proceeded to an Indian Sikh Temple, a Malay village, and a rubber plantation. Brad especially liked the Royal Selangor Pewter factory. He watched as a Malaysian woman factory worker was hammering large decorative dents in the side of a pewter dish. As the tourists walked by, her head remained in the same position, and her eyes never strayed from the pewter dish. She was a veritable robot, expressionless and perfunctory.

Next on the tour was a visit to Batu Caves, reputed to be 400 million years old. The tour guide warned the old folks, "It is a long climb to the caves, 257 steps, so you might wish to remain here and visit the shops."

That is exactly what the shopkeepers wanted. Brad wanted the exercise so he climbed the steps to see the caves.

Last stop on the tour was the Batik fabric factory with a few shops near the entrance. After touring the factory the tourists wandered in and out of the shops. Outside the entrance to one of the shops was a large rectangular wooden box. It was about 12 feet long, six feet wide, and three feet deep.

The tour guide stopped in front of the box and advised his small group, "You must be very careful. You may look over the edge, but do not place your arm into the pen. There are hundreds of scorpions inside. They can't escape, but they can sting you if you reach in."

Several of the tourists in Brad's group walked single file past the pen to see the scorpions. Brad always brought up the rear on tours, and when leaving an airplane. He didn't like being in the middle of a crowd. And by this time he was not anxious to browse through any more shops. The last of the group had already entered the shop as he stopped to look down into the pen. There were several layers of scorpions squirming around, and crawling all over each other on the mossy bottom.

Then he felt a pair of hands on his back pushing him up and over the top of the pen. His head was shoved down until his face was only 12 inches from the incited scorpions. They became frantic upon his intrusion into their territory. One vicious monster of a scorpion leaped up trying to reach Brad's nose with his lethal stinger. Brad shuddered as he came one inch from his target.

Brad grabbed the side of the pen with both hands and thrust his right foot backward into the groin of the assailant, knocking him away. As Brad pushed himself up and out of the pen, he saw the man scamper away, with a slight limp. Brad just slumped to the ground. He was in no mood to pursue anyone, right after meeting an unfriendly scorpion face to face....that is to say.....nose to nose!

The tour guide came out of the shop to smoke a Camel. He saw Brad on the ground. "Are you all right, Sir?"

Brad realized that no one had seen what happened. His first reaction was to keep quiet. After the immigration fiasco he was better off not to involve the police. How could he explain what happened? He didn't know yet himself. One thing certain; it was not a robbery attempt. The assailant could easily have taken his wallet from his back pocket.

After the tour he returned directly to the Melia Hotel, ordered room service and reviewed his notes for the seminar yet to come in Singapore. No matter how experienced, and how careful he was, there were always a few rough spots in the delivery of his lectures that needed improvement. It also kept his mind off the distasteful implications of his brush with death.

CHAPTER 10

Monday, July 15, 1996

"Good morning, Professor Kendall. I trust that your seminar was a success." A voice unmistakably that of the Singapore Airlines Stewardess, Hui Ming Lee. He didn't have to wait for her to say who it was.

"Thank you Miss Lee. Yes, except for a delay caused by the immigration officials at the airport, it was a success."
"I assume that George Tong told you that I would call you to arrange for lunch or dinner today. Which do you prefer?"

"Let's see, it's 11:45 now. Could we meet for lunch at about...one o'clock." With Brad given the choice, waiting until dinner time to meet that alluring voice was unthinkable.

"That will be agreeable, Dr. Kendall. Where would you like to meet?"

"Oh, I thought you would.... well, I would really like to try Movenpick Restaurant on Jalan Bukit Bintang. My neighbor in Mackinaw City was formerly a famous Swiss chef so I learned to love Swiss cuisine."

Brad would normally have insisted that she pick the restaurant, but he couldn't take a chance that she might select one that served only spicy Malay food.

Hui Ming replied, "I have once eaten at the Movenpick Restaurant in Toronto. The food was very good."

Brad arrived at Movenpick's a few minutes early to select a cozy spot. The restaurant was not crowded.

Hui Ming Lee was precisely on time. Every head in the restaurant turned as the Singapore Girl, easily identified by her colorful high-necked Mandarin gown, her short black bangs, and bright red lips, entered the front door.

Her arrival stirred a flurry of activity. Four waiters escorted her to the table, bowing as to a Goddess. Two of them competed to pull out her chair, ignoring Brad's very existence. He shooed them away a little less than politely.

They both selected Movenpick's famous buffet. It was replete with gourmet European selections to the delight of Brad. Hui Ming, as expected, had a thin appetite to match her figure.

They settled back to the table with their plates. "First, I would like to call you Hui Ming.... if.... you will call me Brad. No doctor or professor."

"It is not easy for me, Mr. Bradley, but I will do it to please you."

"No mister either, just Brad, please?" He reached out

and inadvertently touched her hand. She responded with a gentle squeeze. Her smile radiated warmth across the table. He noticed that even the ice in his water glass had melted rather quickly. Just sitting across from this Goddess of Beauty made it difficult for Brad, or for that matter any man, to concentrate on mere words.

Recognizing the situation, very common for her in the presence of men, Hui Ming became businesslike. "I understand.... Bradley," she partially acquiesced, "that you had difficulty with the immigration officials at the airport?"

"Yes, they gave me a hard time for apparently no reason. I'll tell you about it, if you would like."

Hui Ming didn't let him continue. She humbly confessed, "I am responsible for your delay at the airport."

She waited for his reaction, knowing that it would be a shock. Brad's trance over Hui Ming's beauty ended abruptly.

"You.... you mean to say that you were responsible?" Brad's disbelief was ostensible. "But, why? I lost some valuable time from the seminar."

Hui Ming humbly, but tenaciously continued, "You recall that you were scheduled to arrive at Subang International Airport at 1:00 p.m. on Friday."

Brad made the slight correction, "Well, it was 12:55, I believe. But that's not important. Go on."

"I received a call at 12:15 that you were to be kidnapped. A taxi would pick you up at the airport. The driver would say that he was sent by the Pacific Rim Institute. You would be taken to a ship at the harbour, murdered, and your body thrown out at sea."

Stunned by the revelation, he muttered to himself, barely audible, "Oh my Goodness!"

Hui Ming continued. "But I couldn't get to the airport in time. Fortunately I know a high official in the Kuala Lumpur immigration service. He has a fondness for me. He sends gifts to me, and wants me to be his mistress."

She digressed as if she wanted Brad to think about that. "I only tell you this.... so you will understand how I could ask such a favor of him."

She hesitated a moment as if to verbalize carefully. "But I do not repay favors with.... with what most men seem to want from me."

Brad reached out and ever so gently touched her hand and said, "I am sure that you don't."

She smiled and continued. "My friend ordered the immigration officer at the clearance gates to detain you at the airport for at least 30 minutes. I then arrived with another of my admirers, who is a taxi driver. We hoped that the.... what you Americans call a hit man, disguised as a cab driver, would be confused when you didn't exit the airport on schedule."

"We expected that he would drive off to obtain further instructions. But we didn't know for certain.... so we had to intercept you, before he picked you up. My taxi driver and I followed you from the immigration to the baggage area. He had his taxi ready to pick you up when you walked out the door."

"My gosh.... you saved my life, Hui Ming. How can I ever thank you enough?" Brad knew how he would like to thank her, but reaching across the table and giving her a big kiss would not be dignified. And it might smear her impeccable makeup.

Hui Ming added, "The immigration officials at the airport didn't know why you were being detained, so they followed their normal procedure to force you to report downtown. That was not my intention, but there was no way to explain to them our reasons for detaining you. I hope you will forgive me for your delay in the seminar."

Brad slowly and tenderly said, "You saved my life, Hui Ming. You don't have to apologize for anything. I am forever grateful."

At those words, and in spite of her infallible self- discipline and emotional control, Hui Ming's big brown eyes betrayed her improbable surge of affection. Men were supposed to be immobilized by her almost supernatural beauty, but she had always managed to remain unaffected. She knew that her survival as a sexual icon, representing the epitome of feminine sensuality in the oriental world, depended on it.

She had never met a man who overwhelmed her with such genuine platonic concern. She knew in her heart that it was sincere.... not for those.... favors. This man had touched her very soul, and her eyes revealed it. They sparkled with her delight, subtle and subdued, wanting to spring into reality. But generations of cultural propriety intervened. Her body remained a captive of genteel restraint.

Brad was completely oblivious of the message coming from Hui Ming's beseeching eyes. His big news about the scorpion episode had temporarily taken a back seat to Hui Ming's startling revelations.

He excitedly blurted out, "Hui Ming, someone tried to kill me yesterday. I was on one of those tours...you know... the...I think it's called the country tour. We were near the end of the tour...at the Batik factory...where they have the hand painted fabrics."

"There was a pen of scorpions near the tourist shop. I didn't want to go into any more shops...so I waited outside. I was fascinated by the scorpions. Then...as I was looking into the pen...someone tried to push me over the side."

Now it was Hui Ming's turn to be curious. "Oh how dreadful.... how did you escape from falling into the pen?"

"I was able to stop myself from falling with my legs... then...I managed to kick him...and he just ran away. I must have been dazed for a minute or two."

"Did you see what he looked like? Did you report it to the police?"

"No. And no one else saw what happened, so I decided not to report it. I couldn't describe him. Typical Malaysian clothes, small white turban, average height, what could I say? And what good would it do. The police would just insist that he was a petty thief."

"You were very clever. It would serve no purpose to become entwined in a police case. It could have interfered with your other seminar in Singapore...if you were detained to identify suspects."

"Do you think he was trying to kill me or just scare me, Hui Ming?"

"I am certain that he was attempting to kill you. Even one scorpion sting is painful and dangerous. If you had fallen into the pen, a dozen or more stings would have surely killed you. And from what you described, that is what your assailant intended."

Brad looked curiously into Hui Ming's eyes, finally noticing the almost transcendental power of her affection, and innocently asked, "Why would someone want to kill me?"

"I believe that I know why.... but I do not know all the details, yet. You will need to know as much as possible.... and work with us to stop them. Otherwise they will continue to try to kill you."

"In that case I had better cooperate," Brad agreed.

Hui Ming continued. "This may help you to understand why you are involved. Gordon Roberts invited you to lunch last year at the Melia Hotel because he found out that you were in Kuala Lumpur giving your seminar. I was led to believe that it was merely a coincidence. He told Captain Chung and me that he knew you since you were a boy. We didn't know that you were one of George's associates, too."

"But unfortunately, he and Captain Chung and I were being observed by an international terrorist. Either by him personally, or by his paid killers. The alias he is currently using is Chaw Wi Chan, so that is George's code name for him."

"George says that Chaw Wi Chan, a man known as Kuda, and a ship captain, named Kam Quon, are working together. They are the most clever, devious, and treacherous terrorist team in the world. At the time of our luncheon meeting the three of us were actively trying to spy on Chaw Wi for George."

After stopping for a while to enjoy the buffet, Hui Ming continued, "It is now apparent that because of your presence at that meeting you were assumed to be part of our group. Now both Captain Chung and Gordon Roberts are dead. Do you see why they might be trying to kill you?"

"Yes, but how about you. You must be in danger, too."

"I do not worry. I have many admirers who say they would die for me.... if necessary."

Brad considered that to be just boastful talk by men who think they can get special favors from Hui Ming.

"How about George, does he know everything? Can't he stop all this?"

"George knows most of it, but I haven't had time to report what happened to you at the airport, or what I am expecting to learn soon. Let me explain more. I have another...admirer..."

Hui Ming blushed. "I don't want to sound boastful, but I don't know how else to describe these men who worship the Singapore Girl.... as I was saying, this admirer says he will do anything for me. He used to bother me on the plane, the Jakarta to Singapore flight. He threatened to kill himself if I do not go out with him. So I let him take me to dinner once in a while. He is President of a small electronics plant in Penang. He has been supplying certain products to a company called Raja Putra, Ltd., located in Johore Bahru, Malaysia, just across the bay from Singapore. George found out that Raja Putra, Ltd. is owned by Chaw Wi Chan's terrorist group. They have many company names. But George's computerized Information Network System, the INS, can trace the group's activities."

Brad's concentration was periodically sidetracked by the inveigling power of Hui Ming's beauty and charm. He had to force himself to listen carefully.

She continued, "What I try to say is that this admirer.... I do not wish to reveal his name.... he has become more to me.... he is my friend. He will do anything for me. George has given him a code name, Mr. Ikan. He is the one who keeps me informed of Chaw Wi's activities. He is the one, not George, who told me you would be kidnapped. He has recently uncovered a plot against the United States. Maybe to blow up White House. Maybe to kill many Americans. He only say that it is terrible. He will tell me more about it in Singapore. Then.... you and I must meet in Singapore before you return to Honolulu next Monday. George says you must personally carry details of the plot to him. No other way is safe."

Brad was overwhelmed by all this. They stopped talking to enjoy the food for a while. It was 3:10 p.m. They had been talking for over two hours. He had been in the company of one of the most beautiful creatures in the world, and what did they talk about. The theater, music, art, literature, love? No! They talked about unsavory people and insidious plots. What a shame!

Before departing Hui Ming said, "Be very careful during the remainder of your stay in Kuala Lumpur. There are several SIA flights to Singapore each day. On Wednesday, go to the airport one hour earlier and ask to change your flight to No. 132 about ten minutes before flight time. I will make sure that you get on that flight."

Hui Ming said she would leave the restaurant first, alone, and that Brad should leave ten minutes later. She had no intention of alarming him with the details of the dangerous position into which she had been inextricably drawn. But she couldn't hide the plaintive look on her face as she said goodbye.

CHAPTER 11

On Wednesday afternoon Brad flew from Kuala Lumpur to Singapore, following Hui Ming's instructions. The talkative cab driver, who picked him up at the Changi International Airport, tried desperately to get him on a tour.

"Singapura means Lion City, you know, sir. It officially became a city by order of King George VI in 1952. Then, in 1963, it became independent from Britain, and joined with Malaysia. Neither side was happy with that, so Singapore became a separate nation in 1965. Would you like to tour the city, sir? I could pick you up at the hotel."

Brad explained that he taken the tours before. He stopped at the desk of the Carleton Hotel, checking in at 4:45 p.m. His room, reserved again by Balbir Singh, Director of the Pacific Rim Institute, was on the 14th floor over-looking the historic three-story Raffles Hotel. Rudyard Kipling, Somerset Maugham, and Elizabeth Taylor all loved the elegant British hotel. Brad was amazed by the door-man at the circular drive in front of the Raffles. He looked to be about seven feet tall, with his turban. He looked ex-actly like the Punjab in Little Orphan Annie.

Brad relaxed a bit, had dinner alone at the Wah Lok Restaurant in the Carleton Hotel. The Wah Lok was fairly expensive because it was listed as one of the top Cantonese restaurants in Singapore. Brad loved the Cantonese food back home. The waitress did not speak or understand English very well, very uncommon in Singapore. But the menu fortunately had Peking Duck, one of Brad's favorites, so he didn't have to say much, just point. It was one of the cheap-est selections, only S $20.00. Brad quickly used his mental calculator to convert to US $14.00. Sounds great he con-cluded, and pointed his order to her. He didn't have to pay for his meals at the hotel, but he couldn't stop being a money conscious accountant. She repeatedly bowed and said, "Zank you, Zank you."

The maitre d' was standing by and interrupted. "Sir, I do not like to interfere, but I noticed that you are a hotel guest....may I venture to guess, an American?"

"Why yes I am."

"And sir, you pointed to the Peking Duck, did you not?"

"Why yes I did."

"Before your order is placed, sir, I would like to inform you that the Peking Duck served here is quite different from that served in Chinese style restaurants in the United States."

"Oh that's all right. I don't mind a little change. I really do want to try some of the different foods while I'm here."

"Fine sir, but in our Peking Duck all the succulent meat is extracted and only the fat and skin are served. I would suggest this entree, sir. It has a variety of delicious items and is designed specifically for hotel guests." He pointed to a menu item, priced at S $50.

Brad said, "Thank you very much. Please tell the waitress that I will order the one you suggested."

Brad was pleased that the entree was indeed delicious, but for US $35 it ought to be! Perhaps it was just the thought of duck fat and skin that made him enjoy the variety dishes so much.

Thursday, July 18, 1996

The enchanting voice of Hui Ming greeted Brad on the room phone at 8:45 a.m.

"Good morning Professor Kend.... I am sorry. Good morning Bradley."

"Good morning Hui Ming." He gave up on persuading her to call him Brad. Bradley was better than nothing.

"I will have meeting I told you about soon, maybe later today or tomorrow. You must meet me Sunday night in Bugis Village on Bugis Street. Do you know where it is?"

Brad just loved the sound of Bugis, pronounced like boogy. "Yes it is only a few blocks down North Bridge Road to Bugis Street from here. What time?"

"Go to the Bugis Seafood and Shark's Fin Restaurant at 8:30. Sit at any table. A hawker named Boon Huan will look for you. The hawkers have name tags, so make certain it is Boon. He will take you to me."

Hui Ming hesitated. Her voice became melancholy, almost passionate. "I will not be dressed the same. I do not want to be bothered by those.... admirers! We will not discuss any business. I want to be.... only with you. We will have a good time. I will teach you to eat Shark's Fin."

Then her voice rose in excitement. "There is a disco called the Ding Dong A-go-go. We will dance and.... you will hold me tight.... and then.... we will....! I mean that I want to know you better.... before.... before you go. I must see you.... I must.... oh, please forgive me!"

Brad's heart skipped a beat. He was too spellbound to notice the hint of desperation in her voice. But as expected, his academic self-control mitigated his response.

"It would be nice to set business aside for my last evening here, Hui Ming. Thank you for wanting to be with me."

Brad considered it a special honor that a Singapore Girl would want to have what might be called a date with him. In Singapore it would be like going out with a movie star.

He said, "I am taking the harbour cruise on the Admiral Cheng Ho at three o'clock today. I would love to have you come with me."

"I would love to be with you.... more than you will ever know. But I have very important day ahead. I must be ready. You know why, Bradley."

Brad almost melted every time she said Bradley. He

had always preferred Brad, and never liked the sound of Bradley before. But from her lips it sounded heavenly.

"Oh, I'm sorry Hui Ming. Of course I know. Please don't be offended with my familiarity, but I can't wait to see you on Sunday night. I can't think of anything else but you."

"I am pleased with your familiarity. But we must wait. I am anxious to see you, too." Then she strangely said, "I have never been more anxious for anything, Bradley.... but, we must wait."

～～

Brad found the friendly taxi driver, Mohammed's, card. He was pleased to drive Brad to the docks where he boarded the Admiral Cheng Ho at 10:30 a.m. for the Morning Glory cruise. The Cheng Ho was a magnificently beautiful Chinese Junk, decorated with huge wooden carvings. They cruised slowly out of the harbour toward Kusu Island. The small island is sacred to both the Taoists and the Malays. It is named for a mythical turtle, turned into an island to save drowning sailors.

The Singapore Harbour is the busiest in the world. At the Straits of Mackinac in front of the family cottage, Brad saw lots of foreign ships. But they went by one at a time. It was quite a different sight to see hundreds of foreign freighters, anchored in the crowded Singapore Harbour. The Cheng Ho had to carefully maneuver in between or around them. Brad enjoyed the cruise, but something was missing. He knew what it was. He couldn't get Hui Ming out of his thoughts.

In the afternoon, he had Mohammed take him to where you board the cable car ride to the Island of Sentosa. Brad wanted desperately to visit the old Ford Motor Company factory where the British surrendered to the Japanese in World War II. The cable car ride would have been exciting, and the island had three interesting museums. But he decided not to go, and had Mohammed drive him back to the hotel. Brad lacked that enthusiasm found in sharing the experiences with someone else. He was preoccupied with that yearning…. beckoning voice of Hui Ming.

FRIDAY, JULY 19, 1996

The Friday night and Saturday seminar went well. He received compliments from Balbir and from the delegates. All except one man who expected more of a hands-on type of workshop. Brad explained to him that he couldn't provide a room full of computers. But even the success and the praise left him empty. This was his triumphant moment. The two seminars were over and he could finally relax. But he couldn't relax. Something bothered him. He knew what it was. The haunting vision of the sadness in Hui Ming's sensitive face when they parted in Kuala Lumpur. He began to sense the note of predestination in her last words.

At 7:00 p.m. he had dinner at the Carleton's Club Victoria, a buffet that had a sufficient amount of non-spicy selections. He would love to dine at the Raffles, but not alone. Not without Hui Ming.

CHAPTER 12

SUNDAY, JULY 21, 1996

F inally, it was Sunday. The day passed slowly. Brad had only one thing on his mind, Bugis Street, tonight, and Hui Ming. He read about Bugis Village in the Singapore Visitor, a tourist paper. It said that Bugis Village was restored to resemble the original infamous transvestites paradise. It now features souvenir shops and open-air food stalls. Each shophouse had terracotta tiled roofs, edged in bottle green, with ceramic pilasters, (whatever they are.... Brad thought).... and a central Venetian window. The ethnic restaurants have salesmen, called hawkers, who mingle in the crowds to persuade the tourists to dine at their restaurant. They pass out their personal card to receive a commission for customers they attract. There is a market called the pasar malam, and the disco dance hall, the Ding Dong A-go-go, that Hui Ming had mentioned.

He walked in the steamy tropical air for three blocks down North Bridge Road to Bugis Street. Then he turned on Bugis Street to walk a short distance to Bugis Village. He passed through the pasar malam market, looking at the foods. Brad could never understand how meat could sit out in the open air, tropical at that, and be safe. But the open markets were everywhere in Singapore and certified to be safe by virtue of frequent and strict inspections.

A hawker shouted something at Brad, and handed him his card. The card read, Jadeland Restaurant, specializing in Black Pepper Crab, Chilli Crab, and Sambal Pomfret. The name of the Hawker on the card was, Sunny, not Boon.

Brad pushed on through the crowd to sit at a small round table in front of the Bugis Seafood and Shark's Fin Restaurant. It was now exactly 8:30. He was nervous. For almost three days, since Thursday afternoon, he had been uneasy. Very important things, like the seminar's success, the tour of the harbour, seemed to be insignificant. He just wanted to see Hui Ming.

He certainly could not be in love with her; he was just hypnotized by an image. She was the mysterious aura of Asia. She represented all the goodness in Asia, polite and respectful. She was clean. Her dress was always pressed and neat. She had a classic face; her hair never out of place. She was too perfect to be real. He couldn't be in love with that. It was like worshiping a mythological goddess.

Then why was he so anxious to see her. Why did his

heart pound so. Why did he remember her every word, "We will dance and.... and.... you will hold me tight.... and then.... we will....!"

A young hawker approached his table, separating him from his sentimental thoughts. The name on his card was, Boon Huan.

"Are you Professor Bradley Kendall? I am Boon."

"Yes, I am. Hui Ming said you would take me to her."

"Yes I will, but first she said to give you this." Boon handed Brad a small bag.

"What is this? Where is she?"

Boon didn't know what was in the bag. Brad became impatient. Boon led Brad through a back doorway into the narrow lane.

"She told me she would be waiting for you at the back door of the disco. It is at the end of this lane. See the lights down there." Boon pointed to the very end of the lane. Then he hesitated.

Brad knew what he wanted. He pulled out a Singapore ten dollar bill and handed it to him. Boon thanked him and disappeared into the darkness.

Brad walked cautiously down the dark alley toward the back of the Ding Dong A-go-go disco. About half way to the disco, in the darkest area in the lane, he noticed something strange in the trash bin behind one of the buildings.

A horrible fear struck him when he saw that it was the bloody torso of a woman. The upper part of her bruised body was partially covered by waste paper and cardboard. He slumped to his knees and struggled to remove a layer of filthy paper from the recognizable face. He shuddered and wept.

It was the face of his Hui Ming. The beautiful, sweet, innocent Hui Ming Lee. He did fall in love with her. He did. But it was more than physical love. It was spiritual. As if she were an angel who came to intercept the death meant for him. She seemed to know her destiny.

As he was kneeling over her and praying for her, he instinctively, foolishly, wishfully, desperately, reached toward the middle of her back as if searching for the wind-up key. There must be a key that he could use to wind up his Singapore Girl, the China Doll of his dreams, and make her walk and talk again. But the key wasn't there.

When he recovered from the immobilizing period of grief, he grabbed her purse. It was empty, completely empty. He threw it down. The bag.... she knew what might happen. He reached in his pocket to make sure the bag was there. Then Brad, sobbing softly, symbolically threw her a kiss, and slipped away.

As he was walking back to Bugis Village to disappear into the crowds, he opened the bag. Inside was a computer disc. That was all. She had to die for this disc?

He walked the three blocks back to the Carleton Hotel, and went directly to his room. It was 9:25. He tried to be as inconspicuous as possible. After a shower, he watched the local English spoken news, as if he expected a report on the murder. He was distraught and confused. He couldn't sleep, so he watched the CNN international news station.

When he settled down a bit, Brad's analytical accounting mind began to review what had happened. Thank heaven that his plane would leave at 7:10 a.m. And that he would arrive in Honolulu at 6:50 a.m. the same day, because of crossing the International Date Line.

He presumed that the Singapore police would find the body tonight or tomorrow morning. That means they would probably begin investigating tomorrow, and Brad would be safely back in Honolulu. George would protect him if he were traced to the murder in any way.

Now, who would have seen him with Hui Ming? There's the waiters at the Movenpick Restaurant in Kuala Lumpur. They certainly would remember that Singapore Girl dining with a foreigner. But Hui Ming had never eaten at that Movenpick before, so they didn't know her name. And all Singapore Girls are dressed, and made up, to have the same general appearance.

Most important is Boon Huan, who knew Brad's full name. Brad felt confident that the police wouldn't get around to Boon Huan until a day or two. He would probably not offer any information unless pressed by the police. He would not want to be a suspect in a murder. Only if he were accused or implicated would he point to the American professor.

After concluding that there was a low probability of being detained before morning, Brad placed a call to George, who had given him a special number for emergencies. George answered the phone himself, to Brad's relief.

He started to relate the details to George, "Hui Ming was murdered.... before I could talk to her. I have something.... a computer disc.... but I don't know ...."

George said, "Don't say any more. Just continue your return travel schedule exactly as it stands. Go to your friend Billy's as you planned. If everything is clear, I will call you there to arrange our meeting. In the meanwhile my team will follow the news reports, and will be tracing the activities of all of Chaw Wi's hit men. I promise you that we will identify the killer of Hui Ming. You were right to call me, Bradley. If your flight plans are changed in any way, you will know that I am responsible. It will mean there is danger."

"Thank you, George, I feel better now that you know what happened. And I apologize for not telling you that my name, along with the other three, was on that note left behind at the bombing. I always assume that you know everything. But in this case I should have mentioned it. Now they are all dead except me."

"Well, this is one time I didn't know.... but the important thing is that I know now."

Brad was finally relieved enough to get some sleep. Not much, however, with an early morning flight. He called Mohammed's taxi, checked out of the Carleton, and caught the flight without a hitch.

♒

The United flight arrived at Tokyo Narita Airport at 2:55 p.m. on July 22. His flight was scheduled to leave Narita at 6:40 p.m. and arrive in Honolulu at 6:50 a.m. on the same day, July 22.

The Japanese female voice spoke perfect English, slowly and deliberately. Brad thought the announcers in some American airports could use some training from the Japanese. "Dr. Bradley Kendall, please report to information area 10A." She repeated the message as Brad approached the desk. It sounded just like a recorded message, but it couldn't be.

A neatly dressed Japanese hostess handed him an envelope. "Here are the tickets you requested. You will be flying on Northwest Flight 622 to San Francisco. You are assigned to seat 25A. Your flight will depart from Gate 5, at 5:45 p.m. You should arrive at the gate 30 minutes early. From there you are ticketed to Chicago, and then on to Lansing, Michigan. You should examine the tickets for the times, and the seat assignments for those flights. Do you have any questions?"

Brad wanted to say, "Are you kidding? What more could I ask?" And he wanted to say that he didn't request any tickets, but he remembered what George said. A change means possible danger.

The passenger loading gates were all in a wide semicircle, with the ticket and information booths in the center. All of the gates were accessible within a few minutes, one of the few positive aspects of Narita. As he sat down to wait he opened the ticket envelope. There was a small piece of paper inside with a note. It simply said, " Call me when you reach Lansing." No name.

Brad was terribly disappointed about bypassing Honolulu. He was so anxious to see Billy, and he especially wanted to see Alina. She was the right person to comfort him after what happened. And he looked forward to swimming in the ocean and just relaxing at Billy's place.

He looked at all the times of departure and arrival. The International Date Line difference would be minus 24 hours. The flight time and waiting times, including a long wait in Chicago, would be plus 25 hours, and the time change would be plus 12 hours. That explained his arrival in Lansing at 6:45 a.m. on Tuesday morning, July 23.

CHAPTER 13

B rad landed in Lansing on schedule. By 7:30 a.m. he loaded his bags into his 1993 blue Buick LeSabre, retrieved from the long-term parking area. He left the parking lot and turned the wrong way, west instead of toward his apartment in East Lansing. He was heading, his mouth watering, toward Cracker Barrel. They finally built one in Lansing, but it was on the wrong side of town for him. After two weeks of oriental food, the Cracker Barrel's aroma of smoked ham, with good old American cookin' from the deep South, was all he could think of. He ordered his favorite breakfast, two eggs, bacon, sausage gravy on biscuits, and grits.

After stopping for his favorite Primo Lavado coffee at a

Meijer's store, and just a few groceries, he arrived at his apartment on Hagadorn Road. It was nothing special, a standard two bedroom apartment. His parents retired to Florida two years ago, and decided to stay there all year instead of driving back and forth. So Brad had the cottage in Mackinaw City whenever he wanted. He was planning on living there most of this summer, right after the Singapore seminar. It was perfect for doing his research for articles and books.

He waited until three o'clock in the afternoon to call George, which in Michigan daylight savings time would be nine in the morning in Honolulu.

"I'm home in East Lansing, George. I didn't question the changes in my flight schedule. I just assumed that you did it, and had a good reason."

"Yes, you were wise to follow my arrangements. I'll explain why."

"Before you do. Should I call Billy? He was expecting me to spend a few days with him."

George said, "Don't worry. I explained everything to Billy, and he will tell Alina." George seemed to know that Alina would be expecting him too.

"The reason you were derailed was mainly a precautionary one. We traced a terrorist to both Kuala Lumpur and Singapore during the days that you were there. He is a professional killer working for Chaw Wi Chan and Captain Quon's terrorist group. He is listed as Konji Kuda, the Vice-President of Marketing for the Raja Putra, Ltd. We have given him the code-name of Kuda. He was traced to the Country Tour you took in Kuala Lumpur."

Brad had to ask, "Is he the one who pushed me into the scorpion pen?"

"Not exactly. The *New Straits Times* reported that a young Malaysian, a petty thief type, was found with a broken neck on Monday, the day after you took the tour. Kuda is an iron man and specializes in snapping necks. Our guess is that Kuda hired the Malaysian, and killed him after he bungled the job. In fact, he probably would have done away with him either way."

"Did he.... ?" Brad stammered. "Did he kill Hui Ming?"

George answered, "We don't know for sure. Kuda flew to Singapore on Saturday, the day before Hui Ming was killed. Her murder made the headlines in the *Singapore Straits Times* on Monday. The whole city, or should I say nation of Singapore, is up in arms. The police said that she was beaten.... and that her neck was broken. They have no clues at all. They want to interview a hawker in Bugis Village, who was the last one to see her, but cannot locate him."

"We, that is, the INS, has a team member in Singapore. But I have to confess that Hui Ming was the only person who knew his identity. She would not reveal it to anyone, in order to protect him. Did Hui Ming say any thing about her informer to you?"

Brad said, "Why yes, she said there was an admirer of hers who had threatened to kill himself if she wouldn't go out with him. So she went to dinner with him a few times.

When she found out that he knew Chaw Wi Chan she went with him on a regular basis. He said he would do anything for her, and he apparently did.... he told her what he heard at his meetings with Chaw Wi and his group. I think he's your inside man."

George spoke with hesitation. "Now I am gravely concerned. One of the news stories on Hui Ming's murder stated that a man, whose identity was withheld, had committed suicide because of the death of the Singapore Girl."

Brad said, "I hope it wasn't our man. He's the only one who can help us."

George asked, "What else did Hui Ming tell you at your meeting? She had to stop passing me information because she was afraid of being monitored. She was going to tell you anything new."

Brad said, "She hinted at some kind of a plot against the United States. It sounded strange.... she said there was a plot.... maybe to blow up the White House, or to kill a large number of Americans. He was going to tell her about it in Singapore, and she would tell me on the night that she was murdered. She wanted me to carry the details of the plot to you."

George was noticeably disappointed. "You mean she never had a chance to tell you."

"No, she didn't, but she had a hawker, named Boon Huan, contact me at Bugis Village to take me to her at a disco dance club near by. He handed me a package with the computer disc in it. That's all I have. Do you suppose...."

George didn't let him finish, "You may be in serious danger, Bradley. The hawker at Bugis Village must have been this Boon Huan. It didn't mention a name in the news article on Hui Ming's death. But if he is missing, you know what that means."

"I'm afraid I do. If Chaw Wi or Kuda kidnapped Boon Huan, they will easily find out that he gave something to me."

"And then they will kill him," George added. "I have already asked Billy Chin to go to Singapore as quickly as he can to establish a new team there. I'll inform him of Hui Ming's admirer and about Boon Huan, in case he can protect him." That worried Brad. He hated to have his friend Billy in danger, too.

"Oh, another thing," Brad remembered, "about Sam Green, an FBI agent. He's the one who told me about the paper that had the four names on it. He seemed to know about your group. In fact, he asked me if I were still working with you. I thought that was strange. Just how much does he know about all of this?"

George said, "We have a mutual system of cooperation with the FBI. We make our computerized tracing system available to them, and they protect our members in danger. Sam was the agent in your area who was given inside information because of your involvement in the INS. If you were ever in danger, because of your voluntary work for us, he was assigned to protect you. In fact, because of your present dangerous situation, he should be contacted right now."

"Is it all right if I call him? He and I are friends."

"Why yes, he is right there in Lansing. It would be perfect."

"But, is there anything I shouldn't tell him?"

"Let me think.... no....you should explain everything that happened to you. In order to protect you he should know everything. From the cooperation he has given us so far he would make a good team member."

George added, "I noticed that you didn't mention what was on the computer disc, Bradley."

"Oh, I'm sorry, George. I just arrived home today. I had already taken my desk top computer up to the cottage in Mackinaw City before I left for the seminar. I don't have another computer, and I didn't want to use someone else's for this. I'll drive up to Mackinaw sometime tomorrow. So as soon as I get there I'll find out what's on the disc and call you. What time is best?"

"Any time from noon on is best. Now listen carefully, Bradley. You are extremely important to Chaw Wi and his group. They want you dead. They have already tried to kill you, as you well know. I hate to sound callous, but we need you alive as much as they want you dead. So you must protect yourself at all costs."

Brad called the number that Sam Green had given him; no answer other than the taped voice with the usual.... at the ding dong.... message. Brad left the usual response. That night, Brad ate at his mother and dad's favorite restaurant, Bill Knapps, near the Meridian Mall. They had the best blue cheese salad dressing, and El Cheapo Brad loved their fried chicken dinner special; the one that included the dessert; chocolate layer cake with vanilla ice cream, and hot fudge sauce poured over the top. Scrumptious, and of course, low on calories.

WEDNESDAY, JULY 24, 1996

At last, he was on his way to Mackinaw City. His mouth watered when he thought of the whitefish dinners at Audie's, Darrows, and all the other great family restaurants in Mackinaw. On the way North he usually stopped at the Sugar Bowl, in Gaylord. He loved their Greek lemon rice soup. On the way South he liked to stop at Coyle's in Houghton Lake for their popular buffet.

He stopped at Ken's Village Market in Indian River to pick up some groceries and to say hello to his old school chum, Walt. Driving the last 30 miles was always a time of impatience. The anticipation of turning that curve after mile 334 and first seeing the majestic south tower of the Mackinac Bridge reaching into the blue sky was exhilarating.

You would think that after Brad's ventures into the tropical paradise of Hawaii, the cosmopolitan intrigue of Singapore, and the mystique of Malaysia, Mackinac would be rather mundane. On the contrary, the adventurous excitement of the Strait of Mackinac matched that of the Strait of Malacca, the foreign ships passing under the Mackinac Bridge were from all over the world, just like those in the busy Singapore Harbour, and the historic charm and mystique of Mackinac Island was a match for the enchanting Hawaiian Islands.

He drove down Nicolet Street to the IGA store, picked up some milk and a Cheboygan newspaper, turned right onto the wide and attractive main street, Central Avenue. He was heading for the Mackinaw Bakery to get his salt rising bread, some fresh dinner rolls, and two raisin bagels.

Then he stopped in to say hello to his parents' friends at the Sandpiper. He was shocked when the owner told him that two of the historic restaurants in Mackinaw, Teysen's and Kenville's had closed or relocated. At least Teysen's would still have a gift shop, and Kenville's would open a new restaurant in St. Ignace.

He drove along the water toward the Fort, then west along the lake shore, and pulled into the drive of the nostalgic log cabin that he had enjoyed since boyhood. It was a warm sunny day; the water was deep blue. A pair of Mallards with five baby ducklings were dipping their heads into the water, and the view of the bridge was spectacular. What a greeting!

ᗯᗯ

By 6:00 p.m. all the unpacking was done, and Brad had straightened up the cottage to his satisfaction. He drove down to Audie's, greeted all his old friends, including a waitress he once dated, and gobbled up his usual Whitefish sandwich, tossed salad, and coffee with glee. The Mackinaw City Police Chief, Ben Frayer, was eating with a group of Chamber of Commerce members.

"Hi Ben, have you talked to Reino, up in the Sault lately?"

"A coupla weeks ago. In fact he asked me if I knew when you'd be coming. I said no, of course. Where've ya bin?"

"Oh just in Singapore and Malaysia." Brad immediately realized how cavalier he must have sounded.

"What I mean is.... I had to give a seminar over there. I just finished, and I'm glad to be back in good old Mackinaw."

Ben said, "Why don't you give Reino a call. It seemed like he wanted to talk to you. But, that was a coupla weeks back.... ya know."

"Thanks Ben, I will."

Brad drove home and sat down at the computer and turned on his Word Perfect with Windows. He found the disc from Singapore, and slipped it into the slot. It read:

"My Dearest Hui Ming. This disc is the only copy, and the message was not saved on the hard drive. As you already know, I have been a member of Chaw Wi Chan, Kuda, and Captain Quon's secret group. I became involved after they formed a company named Raja Putra, Ltd., which purchased both parts and finished products from my electronics company in Penang. Raja Putra didn't actually manufacture anything, but carried on an enormously expensive secret research project. It was a front for passing on legally made products to illegal buyers. They supplied some illegal weapons to Iraq and to Libya. The electronic triggering devices came from my plant.

When I found out, I threatened to stop selling them products, even though I made huge profits. But they blackmailed me. Before I knew about their illegal operations, they requested that my plant ship direct to the buyers, which was not an unusual procedure. The buyers had fictitious names, and could be easily traced to the illegal countries.

Chaw Wi and his group had the documents that pointed to my company as being responsible for the illegal sales. And our excessive profits were evidence against us. So out of desperation, I cooperated fully with them. Chaw Wi Chan and Kuda now consider me a loyal member of their terrorist council, and I attend all of their secret meetings.

Millions of dollars were sent in from foreign sources that funded the research and the terrorist activities. At the last meeting Chaw Wi announced that the research project was finished, and was a success. They have invented some kind of a new bomb, small enough to carry on a back pack. Chaw Wi said that, with the help of Captain Quon, he and Kuda can place it almost anywhere in the United States. A time and place have been selected, known only to Chaw Wi and Kuda.

Chaw Wi laughed, when he was telling me about it, saying that blowing up the *Singapore Soo* with a conventional bomb, was a trial run. He had deliberately picked the *Singapore Soo* in order to dispose of his two most despised enemies, Gordon Roberts and Captain Wayne Chung.

But, my dear Hui Ming, my loyalty changed when I met you. You know how I worship you. That is why I must warn you. Your life is in grave danger. At the last council meeting, Chaw Wi was suspicious that some information had leaked out. He might suspect me, and he must know that we meet frequently for dinner. So be very careful in passing this information on to your superior, and then, for my safety, destroy this disc."

$$\approx$$

Brad printed one copy on his HP Laser Printer, did not save the file, and destroyed the disc. Then he called George at 11:01 p.m., cheaper rates of course, which is 5:01 in the afternoon in Honolulu. He started to read the message verbatim to George.

George stopped him, "Check your house carefully for any bugs or taps.... do it right now, so that we can be sure no one will hear this conversation.... and remember not to fax me anything.... too easy to intercept. We have complete secrecy on my end, but we can't control your calls to me."

"Okay George, it's dark outside here, but I'll check the phone now, and call you right back."

Brad checked the phone and traced the phone lines to the outside of the house. He found no sign of any tampering. Then he called George back and read the complete message him.

George's response was, "Now we know what they are planning.... but, only in a general sense. We must not lose the whereabouts of Kuda, Chaw Wi, or Captain Quon."

"Are you able to trace them all the time?" Brad asked.

"No. The reason I sidetracked you to Lansing, instead of having you bring the disc to me here, was because just when you took off for Honolulu, we lost track of Kuda. Anyone can elude our computers for short periods of time. He could have tried to kill you anywhere between Singapore and Honolulu. So I made a last minute change.... one he couldn't discover until it was too late.... to send you straight to Lansing. But, keep in mind that now that you are back in Michigan, I can't protect you as easily. So you must be careful."

"Don't worry, I'm in my own back yard here. I have friends who can break Kuda in half, if necessary." Brad was exaggerating, but it made him feel better.

George said, "Bradley, I know you will contact Sam Green, but I want to send Billy there as soon as he is free from his work in Singapore. You need someone with you. He is your friend, so no one will suspect that there is anything wrong. How does that sound?"

Brad was delighted. "I agree. And besides protection, maybe Billy and I together can figure out what their target might be."

"Fine, then it will be done. Keep me informed of anything new over there."

THURSDAY, JULY 25, 1996

On Thursday morning Brad checked again, with the benefit of daylight, for anything unusual around the cottage and found nothing of concern. He called his old friend, Chief Reino Asuma, at the Sault. "Allo Reino, ouw ya bin, ya ol' Finlander you, eh!" Brad tried to sound like a typical Upper Peninsula Finn, but he wasn't very convincing.

"Brad, am I glad to hear from you. And who are you to

kid the Finns. I remember that your mother's maiden name was Kiltonen."

"She wasn't all Finn. She'll never admit it, but her mother was half Swede, and you know how the Finns and the Swedes always kid each other."

Reino got down to business. "When can I see you? Would you like to drive up here, and stay over night with me? Or do you want me to come there?"

"I'd love to drive up to the Sault, Reino. And I'll stay one night, if that's okay? But are you still alone? No girl-friends.... I mean relatives visiting?"

"No, I have plenty of room. I still live in the little old house on Riverside Drive along the St. Mary's."

Brad said, "I have a lot of work to do for a few days, and I don't want to come on a weekend, so I'll be there on Tuesday..... if that's all right?"

"Tuesday's fine. We have a lot to talk about, so don't waste any time coming."

~~~

The phone rang later that afternoon. "Hello Brad, this is Sam. I got your message. I sure hope you have something to tell me about that Chaw Wi guy!"

"I have quite a long story to report. Do you want it over the phone?"

"No, I am on an assignment right now, but I can fly up there in a few days. When's a good time?"

"Well, I'm meeting Reino in the Sault on Tuesday. If

you want to fly into the old Kincheloe Air Base..... they call it Chippewa County Airport, now..... Reino and I will pick you up."

"Let's see, Tuesday.... yep, I can be there, Brad. I'll call Reino, and let him know when I'll arrive. I'm anxious to hear all about your trip. See you then."

CHAPTER 14

The *Kapitan Malaga* was anchored in the busiest harbour in the world, Singapore. The temperature was 87 degrees, the average high temperature in the summer. Close to the Equator, there is almost no variation in the temperature, nor in the hours of daylight. In the morning, Captain Kam Quon had taken a bus over the causeway, from Singapore to the Malaysian city of Johore Bahru. The bus passed in front of the beautiful and stately Royal Abu Bakar Mosque. He was met at the bus station and transported to the offices of Raja Putra, Ltd. The building was inconspicuously located in a small business district.

Inside Chaw Wi Chan and Kuda were sitting in a modern appearing office. On the outside of the door it read:

128

Konji Kuda, Vice-President - Marketing. Kuda was smoking a long black Havana cigar.

"What are you bringing from Hong Kong this trip, Captain?" asked Chaw Wi.

"The usual, clothing. We are loading more from Indonesia and Malaysia in the Singapore Harbour today. We will leave tomorrow morning at eight o'clock."

Chaw Wi asked Captain Quon, "Will we have separate berths this time?"

"Yes, there is adequate room this trip."

Kuda said, "Chaw Wi doesn't like my cigar smoke. He will be happy."

Chaw Wi agreed, "My friend Konji, he wakes up at night and smokes his cigar in that small compartment. You may easily understand why I prefer a separate berth."

Captain Quon, a Camel smoker since he was 16, was not overly sympathetic. He gave an equivocal grunt and asked, "What are the plans? Is this to be the time.... or is this another practice run?"

Chaw Wi answered, "This, my dear Captain Quon is the time. One million, in U.S. dollars, has been deposited in the Raja Putra account. Two more will be deposited after the.... shall we say.... the event."

Captain Quon looked at Kuda, "When I was in route from Hong Kong, I heard about that Singapore Girl who was murdered a few days ago. I hope you had nothing to do with that, Konji?"

"Who would dare to hurt a Singapore Girl? Only a very brave man. No?" Kuda successfully avoided an answer.

"That's the same answer you gave me last March when I dropped you off in Hong Kong, and the next day that rich businessman from Columbia was found in a hotel room with his neck broken."

"But, he was about to double cross our sponsors. The ones who are paying us a million dollars each. Isn't that reason enough?"

"Yes, I know it is a necessity, but I don't have to like it." Captain Quon said.

Although he didn't relish taking part in the grisly deeds of his partners, he couldn't resist the instant wealth. He left the details of the requests from the terrorist leaders up to Chaw Wi and Kuda. He just had to know where and when to sail the *Kapitan Malaga* before and after the strikes were made.

"You still have two more to eliminate, Konji," Chaw Wi said. "You were fooled by that Hawaiian group that continually plagues us. We must find out who they are and destroy them. All we know is that they operate out of Honolulu."

Kuda said, "I know. I waited at Narita for the professor.... and when I found out that he, or someone else, had changed his flight, I flew straight to Honolulu. But no Dr. Bradley Kendall had landed on any of the earlier flights from Tokyo. So I flew right back here. That Honolulu group must have somehow traced my movements. Next time I will fool them. You will see!"

The meeting ended after a few details of the departure were discussed. The next morning, at precisely eight o'clock, the *Kapitan Malaga* sailed out of the bustling Singapore

Harbour. But it carried only one extra passenger, with official identification as a sales representative for the merchandise on board. In a last minute decision, Chaw Wi had decided that Kuda had a more urgent mission. Kuda had taken a taxi to Changi Airport.

TUESDAY, JULY 30, 1996

Brad had the breakfast buffet at the Mackinaw Pancake House and started out for Sault Ste. Marie at 10:30. He drove onto the Mackinac Bridge on a beautiful sunny day. The view from the bridge was spectacular, so clear you could see for miles. On the west he could see an ocean freighter disappearing into Lake Michigan. On the east he could see a 1,000 footer in front of Mackinac Island coming in from the Soo Locks. It looked like the *Stewart J. Cort*, but from this angle and distance he couldn't be quite sure.

There are only thirteen giant lakers, seven sized at 1,000 feet, five at 1,004 feet, and the *Paul R. Tregurtha* at 1,013 feet. The first of the giants was the *Stewart J. Cort*, built in 1972. Brad was a boat watcher and could recognize several of the 1,000 footers at a considerable distance, without binoculars to see the name on the side or the stern.

The *Stewart J. Cort* was easy. All of the 1,000 footers, except the *Cort*, have the pilothouse and crew quarters at the stern, but no cabins at the bow. The *Cort* has a cabin section at both ends. It was built in three places. The bow section was built in one place, the stern in another, and they were transported to Lake Erie where the two end sections were attached to the middle.

So the *Cort* has a three story block with the pilothouse and crew quarters at the bow, and a three story cabin section at the stern. No other laker is built this way. So when Brad saw a 1,000 footer with cabin sections at both ends he knew that it was the *Stewart J. Cort.*

He could also tell the *Presque Isle* by its shape. The *Presque Isle* is a 153 foot tug boat, and a 974 foot self- unloading bulk carrier, built together to a combined length of exactly 1,000 feet. So Brad could distinguish it by the narrow tug boat segment at the stern.

He loved to tell these little anecdotes to the tourist kids, who were amazed by his encyclopedic facade. His favorite one was, "Did you know that if you stood the *Stewart J. Cort* on its end down to bedrock, next to Pier 19 or 20, those are the two tower piers.... it would stick up about 300 feet above the top of the tower. That's the length of one football field. Just try to visualize that! But don't you ever try it without your parents permission."

Brad arrived at Sault Ste. Marie an hour later and drove straight to the Police Station to see Reino. Reino pushed out a massive right hand, "Good to see you, ol' buddy.... or should I say world traveler. How's your nose?"

Brad had no trouble recalling their hockey match when Reino whapped him on the nose. "I think it's still crooked, thanks to you," Brad kidded.

"Hey I got a call from Sam Green, you know, FBI Sam. He said he talked to you and will be here at three."

"I said we would pick him up, Reino. Is that all right? Do you have enough time?"

"Sure, I kept today open to be with you. Now sit down and let's talk for a while, and then we'll go out to lunch. Is an hour okay, or are you hungry now?"

"No, an hour's fine. I had a big breakfast."

"Tell me about your trip to Singapore. It sounds like fun. I'll bet it's hot there."

"It sure is. I love it there, but it's a long, long flight. The round trip is equal to going around the world."

Reino got serious, "I assume that Sam got a hold a you before you left for Singapore."

"Yep, he told me about Chaw Wi Chan and the note with my name on it. That's what I'm going to tell you all about. You won't believe half of it. Especially the scorpions!"

Brad and Reino agreed that it would be better to wait until Sam arrived before relating the details of the Singapore adventure. They had lunch at one of Reino's favorite restaurants, The Studebaker, and then proceeded out to the airport.

"How's your old girlfriend.... what's-her-name?"

"I don't have a girlfriend, Brad."

"Well you know who I mean.... that reporter. You grew up together.... and you're both divorced.... and you live in the same town.... and... I just assumed you still like each other. Am I wrong?"

"She's a pain.... in the.... you know what. But, you're right. I still do like her. But don't ever tell her. I don't want to get involved with anyone just yet." Reino seemed rather serious about it.

The two friends pulled up at the air strip and greeted Sam. They drove back to the privacy of Reino's office so that Brad could relate the details of his recent travels. He deliberately left out Poh Lay's attempt to seduce him with her voluptuous attributes, even though most virile young men would have considered it one of the most delightful episodes to describe. He avoided any implications of his affection for Hui Ming, and Alina was simply described as his friend's sister. They became merely impersonal subjects in his story.

He let each of them read the printed copy he made from the disc.

Sam said, "Let's make another copy of this."

"No," Brad said emphatically. "I have the only copy. We must protect Hui Ming's friend. Only George and we three know what was on the disc."

Reino said, "What do you think of all that stuff about terrorists and the bomb, Sam?"

"As we have been hearing on the news repeatedly, it's not a matter of if any more.... it's when and where the terrorists will strike again in our country. Israel has its terrorists, and Britain has the IRA. But the United States is becoming the most vulnerable country in the world. We have an assortment of potential bombers who might erupt anywhere or at any time."

Reino interjected, "You can play.... I mean.... say that again, Sam!"

They all burst out laughing at the unintended play on words.

"What I was saying before the Bogart pun," Sam continued, "is that our country is so free that it's becoming impossible to stop terrorists. Anyone without a criminal record has complete freedom to assemble an arsenal and to travel anywhere inside the U.S."

"Not only that, "Reino added, "but our advanced technology has made almost anything possible."

Brad just had to get his two cents worth of wisdom in. "And our legal system makes it almost impossible to convict the criminals even if they are caught. So it all adds up to open season on America. But moaning and groaning about all that isn't going to help us now. We have to figure out where Chaw Wi, Kuda, and their Captain Quon are going to strike."

Reino said, "Brad, do you think we can ever locate this guy over in Singapore who gave the disc to Hui Ming?"

"Maybe, if Billy had any success over there. George sent him there to find our mysterious businessman. By the way, George gave him the code name of Mr. Ikan. Hui Ming told me that he is the president of a small electronics plant in Penang. That's in Malaysia, between Singapore and Kuala Lumpur. As we heard on the tape, he has been supplying certain products to this company called Raja Putra, Ltd., which is owned by Chaw Wi Chan's terrorist group. And that's how they blackmailed him into working with them."

Brad added, "But.... George also mentioned that some man.... no name given, had committed suicide, which was assumed to be related to Hui Ming's death. If that man is Mr. Ikan we have lost our inside man."

Reino said, "That's absurd, no smart businessman is going to kill himself over some dame."

Brad's face grimaced. Although inwardly affected, he calmly remarked, "It seems absurd to you, but this man risked his life every day for Hui Ming.... so he might very well have given up his life when he found out that she was murdered. And I must add, although it could be an exaggeration.... Asian men have reportedly committed suicide just because a Singapore Girl turned them down for a date."

Reino responded, "Okay, I could tell the way your face lit up when you described her earlier that she must have been some chick. But let's not be pessimistic.... let's assume that our Mr. Ikan is still alive. And as you say, Billy may have found out something over in Singapore by now. When is he coming.... by the way?"

Brad said, "I don't know, yet. I'll give him a call when I get back to Mackinaw."

Sam wanted to go over all the details once again before they parted. When Brad got to the part about the tour, Reino blurted out, "Tell us about those scorpions again, Brad. How close did that big one get to your nose. Did you say it was only one inch? Now if I had been there, I would have loaned that scorpion my hockey stick!"

They all laughed, even though Brad's visualization of the incident wasn't too funny. Reino invited Sam to have dinner with them and Susan, but he had made arrangements to fly back to Detroit before dark.

Reino wanted to go to another of his favorite restaurants, the Antlers, which was on Portage Street along the

St. Mary's River. Antlers was popular because it had animal trophies everywhere. As you walked in you were greeted by a seven foot stuffed polar bear. Up in the rafters were three lions, black and brown bears, moose and bison heads. Its history goes back before Prohibition Days when it was originally named the Bucket-of-Blood Saloon and Ice Cream Parlor. During Prohibition it served as a front, selling only one quart of ice cream a month, and refusing to sell their special blend of lemonade to minors.

Susan Young met them at seven o'clock. Brad couldn't help but notice how attractive she was. With her short, neatly waved, blonde hair, she was obviously of Scandinavian ancestry. Brad knew the look.... probably a Swede-Finn. After all the Swedes dominated Finland for 600 years.

Reino said, "Do you remember Brad, Susan?" He's from Mackinaw City. We played hockey against each other as kids, and later we became good friends."

"Nice to meet you, Brad. Reino has told me a lot about your illustrious career."

"I don't know what he has told you Susan, but it couldn't be all good."

Reino said, "Brad, I have kept Susan up to date. She has promised to be discreet.... and I know we can trust her. If not I told her I wouldn't marry her!"

"Oh you dumb lug, I wouldn't marry you if you were the last man on earth." Susan countered.

"Just kidding!" Reino admitted. "But, seriously, I want Susan to work with us. She can be helpful."

"Sure, as long as you realize, Susan, that secrecy is a

matter of life and death. A year ago, I was just having lunch with a few people, and now someone is trying to kill me. So your life may become in danger just by working with Reino and me. I'm sure that's reason to be discreet."

With that settled, the conversation continued on the lighter side. Brad concluding that Susan was indeed the right girl for Reino. He knew that Reino really wanted her on the team so he could spend more time with her. They were both being cautious in cultivating their relationship because of their previous failed marriages.

The three friends chatted at Reino's house for a while. Susan said her goodbyes. Brad spent the night with Reino and departed for Mackinaw the next morning.

CHAPTER 15

MONDAY, AUGUST 5, 1996

Senator Graham Fleming, from California, was the over whelming favorite, by virtue of the primaries, for the presidential nomination at the San Diego Republican Convention, which was to begin on August 12th. It was no surprise when he announced that he wanted the popular Michigan Governor Dan Broadwell for his running mate. Senator Fleming was a Navy Captain in the Korean War and had worked for the CIA during the 1960s. He wouldn't discuss any details about his assignments, in spite of the over-rambunctious reporters who would love to pick up any tidbit of news, good or bad.

Governor Broadwell was an avowed conservative and very successful in instituting new daring programs in Michigan. He was selected by Senator Fleming because he was respected nationally for his success in lowering taxes and fighting crime. In 1995 he had invited the Republican leaders to Mackinac Island for a major strategy meeting. Governor Broadwell managed to keep the meetings so quiet that the national press coverage was almost absent, which was a political miracle in itself.

"Hello Sam, this is Dan Broadwell."

Sam was in the FBI office in Lansing, close to the Capitol Building. His headquarters was in Detroit, but he spent just as much time in Lansing because it was the state capital.

"Do you mean Governor Broadwell, or Vice-President Broadwell?"

"Don't count my chickens before.... you know the rest, Sam. Right now it's just the Governor. I'm going to need you soon."

Sam was assigned to supervise the security of the Michigan Governor. And now that Governor Broadwell was the favorite for the nomination as Republican Vice-Presidential candidate, Sam's job was going to escalate.

"Sam, I am going to invite all 31 of the Republican Governors to Mackinac Island on August 30 for two days. That's on a Friday. Then on Saturday Senator Fleming will fly in and give a rallying speech.... to get them all to back him in the presidential race.

"Labor Day is the following Monday. The governors will have to be back in their states for Labor Day, so they'll all leave on Sunday. But Graham has agreed to walk the

Mackinac Bridge with me. This time we'll arrange to have maximum news coverage."

Sam said, "That means a lot of security. You'll need more with a presidential candidate."

"That's why I'm telling you now. You should get approval for whatever manpower is allowed for candidates in a situation like this. I've invited Graham to come to the Governor's Residence on the Island next Saturday. That's August 10th. The next day he'll fly directly to San Diego for the convention. Can you meet with us say.... at lunchtime?"

"Of course.... I'll be there at noon." Then Sam hesitated, "I was just thinking, Dan. There is something going on that you should know about, and as a presidential candidate Senator Graham should know, too. Would it be all right to bring Brad Kendall? He is a business professor at Michigan State University."

"I've met him at one or two university meetings. He's that international lecturer, isn't he?"

"That's the one. Brad just returned from lecturing in Kuala Lumpur and Singapore, and someone tried to kill him. There's a definite connection with the July 1st bombing at the Soo Locks. This would be a perfect time to brief you."

"Okay then," Governor Broadwell concluded the conversation, "I'll see you and Professor Kendall next Saturday at Mackinac."

WEDNESDAY, AUGUST 7, 1996

"Hello Brad, this is Billy," the cheerful voice from Hawaii said. "Is it okay for us to visit you?"

"I can't wait. You two.... I assume you mean that Alina is coming too.... have never seen Mackinac, have you?"

"No," Billy chided, "and we just can't wait to see the longest suspension bridge in the world, the longest porch in the world, the biggest lock in the world, and the longest lake freighters in the world, etcetera, etcetera, etcetera."

"Do I really sound like that? I guess I do brag a lot about Mackinac," Brad conceded. "When are you planning to come?"

"How about Monday, the twelfth? There is a direct flight from Honolulu to Chicago. Then we can get a flight into Pellston from Chicago. It arrives at 1:30 in the afternoon. How's that?"

"Great, Billy. I'll pick you up. Remember the weather here can turn cool anytime, even in August. Make sure that Alina brings something warm to wear. I don't have any women's clothes around."

"Thanks for the reminder. I'll tell Alina. See you later ol' buddy."

〜〜〜

Sam called Brad and asked if he could meet with Governor Broadwell, Senator Fleming, and him on Saturday. Brad was flattered that Sam would want him for such an important meeting.

On Saturday morning the FBI Lear Jet flew Sam into the former Kincheloe Air Base, 35 miles north of the bridge, and Brad picked him up.

"How can you stand living up here in the summer, Brad?

Isn't it boring in a small town, especially with a bunch of fudgies.... isn't that what they call the tourists.... filling up the streets?"

Brad could have given him the longest bridge and porch in the world spiel, but instead he said, "To each his own, Sam. I don't care for the fast life in a crowded city. And I can do my publish or perish stuff better in a quiet setting."

Brad drove to the Arnold Lines to board the 11:00 a.m. ferry. A streamlined Catamaran was due to dock in five minutes.

"There's Mike. He's the manager, Sam. If you ever need any help, he's the one to see. For that matter, Arnold Lines has a great staff. They're always nice and friendly."

Mike spotted Brad and gave a wave from the office building. They boarded the Island Express for the 18 minute ride to the Island. As they approached the green buoy marking the shipping lane that led directly under the center of the two main towers of the Mackinac Bridge, a freighter was approaching from the east, between Mackinac Island and Round Island.

Brad couldn't hold back his childlike excitement, "Look Sam, there's the *Roger Blough.*"

"How the heck can you tell if it's the *Roger Blough.* I can see the side of the ship from here, but I sure can't read the lettering on the bow."

Brad said, "Well.... it is a guess. But, that ship is as wide as a 1,000 footer. Thousand footers are 105 feet wide. But, it has a stack of cabins at both ends, not just at the stern. The only 1,000 footer built that way was the *Stewart*

J. Cort, which was the first 1,000 footer built. But, it can't be the *Cort* because it's not quite as long a 1,000 footer. So, the only laker that is 105 feet wide, but only 858 feet long is the *Roger Blough*. See!"

In a few minutes they passed close by the huge freighter. Sam could easily read the name printed at the bow, the *Roger Blough*, and USS, Great Lakes Fleet.

"All right, Brad, I'm glad you're on my team."

With his new badge of perfection, Brad proceeded to bore Sam with more of his encyclopedic information.

"During mid-day in July and August there are 12 ferries in motion on the Straits almost continuously, Sam. Every half-hour three ferries, one each from the Arnold Line, the Star Line, and Shepler's, leave Mackinaw City for Mackinac Island. Another three leave St. Ignace for the Island. Six more leave the Island, three headed for Mackinaw, and three for St. Ignace."

Sam yawned and yearned for the landing on the much more exciting Mackinac Island.

"The ferries from Mackinaw City cross two shipping lanes, one with many 1,000 footers traveling between Lake Michigan and Lake Superior. They go directly in front of Mackinac Island and the Grand Hotel on their way to the Soo Locks. The other lane carries all types of ships, including most of the colorful foreign freighters coming from the St. Lawrence Seaway headed for ports like Chicago, Milwaukee and Escanaba. Did you know all that, Sam?"

"Well not really," Sam admitted.

Brad managed to add, just before they landed, "Now

picture a foggy mid-morning in the Straits of Mackinac. The twelve Island ferries are scurrying in all directions.... a 1,000 foot self-unloading laker is heading west, in front of Mackinac Island.... a 750 foot Canadian bulk carrier is heading east, under the Mackinac Bridge.... and a 590 foot foreign freighter is approaching Mackinaw City. Then add ten or twelve skittish private sailboats, dodging the ore boats and ferries. What a ship captain's nightmare, eh, Sam?"

Sam was too interested in the docking to answer. It was a beautiful sunny day. He didn't want to visualize a foggy day. An attractive young lady deck hand climbed through the opened front hatch onto the foredeck and tossed a hawser around the post, while the captain skillfully brought the 350 passenger ferry to a soft nudging along the side of the dock.

Brad had seen this scene many times, but it could never become routine. And Sam, most of his life spent in busy, over-populated cities, with racing cars, honking horns, crowded, noisy restaurants, was in a trance.

The first sight for the awe-filled tourists was a team of two Percherons pulling a dray filled with boxes for the restaurants and gift shops. Everything on the Island has to be transported by horse and wagon, or by bicycle. At the entrance to the dock stood the elegant Grand Hotel coach, waiting for the passengers. The Grand Hotel, built in 1887, stood as a symbol of the uncomplicated past. The entire Island was an adventure into the 19th century.

The only nonsequitur about this venture into the past was the presence of twentieth century tourists in their tight jeans and tee shirts, and their children in their iconoclastic, baggy, clown-like clothes. They were milling around the docks lining up for the next ferry, or watching the huge work horses. Without them the scene would be a nostalgic dream. But then.... how could Mackinac Island flourish without them?

Brad and Sam walked toward Fort Mackinac. The horse-drawn taxis were lined up along Huron Street at the foot of the hill that led up to the fort. Brad decided that they could walk up Fort Street, the steep road on the west side of the fort, and on up to Huron Road. The Governor's Residence was on top of the hill just west of the fort. As they trudged up the hill they could hear tour guides telling the fascinated tourists about Fort Mackinac. That the British had moved Fort Michilimackinac and the entire settlement, what is now called Mackinaw City, over to the Island in 1780, in order to flee those American Revolutionists.

Sam was puffing by the time he reached the top. "You told me it's an easy climb, Brad!"

"We....ll, I thought you were in tiptop shape, Sam."

"I am, but this is really steep; those British must have just rolled down the hill into the fort when they took it back in the War of 1812."

"This isn't the same hill, but you seem to know your history, Sam."

"I've taken the tour, you know.... with the team of those enormous horses, first a two-horse team and then a bigger wagon with four horses. What did you say they were.... Clydesdales or Purchons.... or something?"

"Percherons, but the big ones are Belgians. They usually carry the big wagons. And there are some mixed breed horses, too."

They stopped for a few moments at the top of the bluff overlooking the Straits to appreciate the view, where 1,000 footers and salties, of all sizes, configurations, and colors, pass by every day and night from late March through early January.

Sam said, "Look at that ship with the four masts, or whatever they're called."

Brad said, "That's a saltie, an ocean freighter, see the way it's built. Short, probably 600 or so feet.... and the four derricks and booms... that means it's a general cargo vessel. A bulk freighter, that carries grain.... or iron ore.... would be flat."

"How do you know all this stuff? I suppose you even know where it's from.... I can read the name from here. It's looks like *Ziemia Chelminska*." Sam spelled it out.

"You picked an easy one.... it's from Poland. There is a whole fleet of *Ziemia's* and *Ziemie's* that come in the St. Lawrence. I don't know the difference in the two spellings.... maybe two different Polish fleets."

"And the way I learned was that my Dad loves to watch the ships on the Straits. He wrote some short articles for the local newspaper. They were aimed at the tourists.... not too technical. He told me that he calls his friend, Al Ballert, the foreign ship expert for the Great Lakes Commission down in Ann Arbor, when he needs information on the foreign ships."

"Although it seems improbable, February is the only full month when there is no traffic on the Straits. My Dad's records showed that in 1996 the *Burns Harbor*, a 1,000 foot laker, was seen on January 2 heading east; and the Soo Locks opened on March 25th. And that's the pattern almost every year, depending on the weather, of course."

"I never would have guessed that," Sam admitted. "I thought the ships stopped all winter.... at least three months or so."

"Nope, in fact my Dad spotted the *Kiisla*, a Finnish saltie, trudging slowly along in the Straits just west of the bridge back in February of 1993. The Straits, technically it's the Strait of Mackinac, but Straits just sounds better.... anyway, they were completely covered with ice. The Coast Guard Cutter, *Mackinaw*, was a few hundred yards ahead.... cutting a path through the ship lane."

"Next time he drove to Sault Ste. Marie, my Dad went to the Coast Guard Station to find out how a foreign ship could be in the Great Lakes in February. He knew that the Welland Canal was closed.... and the Soo was closed.... so how the heck could the *Kiisla* get into the Straits? "

"A couple of the officers told my Dad that a foreign ship can't work between two U.S. ports. Some law, I think it's called the Jones Act, prohibits it. But they can ship between a Canadian and a U.S. port. And who do you think has the mightiest ice breakers in the world? The Finns, of course. The *Kiisla's* big.... 600 feet or more.... compared to the 290 foot *Mackinaw*, and its got some fancy ice breaking equipment in the bow."

"So the *Kiisla*, a tanker, could have been transporting chemicals or something from a Canadian port on Lake Huron, like Goderich or Sarnia, to a U.S. port, like Milwaukee or Chicago."

Sam's FBI training didn't fail him. "Then why was the *Mackinaw* cutting a path for the more powerful Kiisla through the Straits?"

"I wondered the same thing, Sam. The Finns aren't so dumb. They probably let the *Mackinaw* cut the path to save the wear and tear on their expensive equipment. But, we'll never know for sure."

CHAPTER 16

B rad and Sam reached the entrance to the modest, but graceful, Governor's Residence. The stately Victorian style home, with eleven bedrooms and eight bathrooms, was built in 1902 for a Chicago attorney. It was purchased in 1944 by the State Park Commission for use as a summer residence for Michigan governors.

Two of Sam's FBI agents appeared suddenly at the bottom of the porch steps. One said, "We were expecting you, Sam. Right on time."

Governor Dan Broadwell opened the door to the main living room replete with Georgia Yellow Pine. "Come in Sam.... and this must be Professor Kendall. Good to see you again."

The Governor held out a hand and said, "This is Senator Graham Fleming. He tells me that you two bumped into each other when he was in the CIA, Sam."

Sam said, "Right. Good to see you again, Senator."

Brad said, "It's an honor to meet with the future president and vice-president of the United States."

Senator Fleming replied, "I have to be optimistic, so I'll just say thank you, Professor Kendall. We really do have high hopes this time if we are nominated.... and if that damn Perot doesn't mess it up again."

Lunch was served by two young women dressed in long nineteenth century gowns. Brad guessed that they probably worked at Fort Mackinac. After lunch, the room was cleared of everyone except the four men.

The Governor began, "I told Sam that I have invited all 31 of the Republican Governors to Mackinac Island on Friday, August 30th for two days. Last year we had a low key strategy meeting at the Island that was very successful. Fortunate for us the media didn't consider it top news. All the top Republican leaders were on hand, so we were able to agree on our goals for the party. We pledged to have another meeting this year to coordinate the campaign strategy."

"Graham has a grueling campaign schedule, so he won't be able to fly in until Saturday to give his pep talk. Then on Sunday the Governors are free to leave. They'll want be back in their own states for Labor Day. And Graham has agreed to walk the Mackinac Bridge with me. So Sam, the FBI has informed me that you'll be in command. You will coordinate all activities of the Coast Guard, the State Police, Bridge Security, and the local police. Does that agree with what you've been told?"

Sam replied, "Correct, Dan. I'll take care of everything. You and Senator Fleming won't have to worry about a thing.... except...." He hesitated and continued, ".... not a thing."

Brad wasn't at all convinced of that last remark. His gut feeling was one of uncertainty.

"Now Sam, what is it you wanted to tell us?" Governor Broadwell asked.

"Because of the upcoming election you two and, of course, the incumbent President, will be the major news of the day. And the threat of terrorism is growing worse all the time. The bombing of that foreign freighter at the Soo Locks has never been solved."

"I know.... I've been pretty upset about that," Governor Broadwell fussed.

"Anyway, Brad and I have a theory. We think we know who did it.... but, we don't know exactly why."

"Can't the FBI do something about it?" Senator Fleming queried.

"No," Sam said emphatically. "It's strictly international, and could never be proved. That's why we want you to know about it. This whole mess involves some Pacific Rim countries, and probably some Middle East countries. The government of Singapore wants to know what happened to the *Singapore Soo*, too. Assuming that, after the convention, you are elected as President, Senator, I want you to know our theory.... just in case we need your support."

"Go on.... go on," the Senator urged.

"Brad will take over from here. He was directly involved."

Brad began, "What Sam means is that he found a piece of paper left behind by the bomber that had my name on it. There were three other names on the slip of paper.... now they are all dead. And someone tried to kill me in Kuala Lumpur."

Brad continued, "The three names on the paper were Captain Chung, Gordon Roberts, and a Singapore Airlines stewardess named Hui Ming Lee. The two men were killed on the *Singapore Soo*."

Brad swallowed and hesitated, "And Hui Ming was murdered in Singapore.... just before...."

Not wanting to explain the Ding Dong A-go-go....Brad stopped to select his words carefully, ".... just before she was going to reveal some information to me."

"I discovered her body.... but I was able to leave without being seen. So, fortunately I was not implicated in any way. If the Singapore police thought I did it, I'm sure I'd get more than four swats with a cane."

Sam intervened, "What Brad is telling you is that there is the possibility of more trouble. Big trouble in the way of terrorism.... and terrorism in the United States. It could be right here in the midwest. We want you to know that we are working with a Hawaii-based group.... the best anti- terrorist operation in the world. In fact it has world-wide cooperation.... to locate the leaders who plan these inhuman acts of terrorism. There are indications that the Soo bombing was small, compared to what these madmen are planning to do next."

Senator Fleming said, "I assume that you are telling

us that this must be kept in absolute confidence until you are more specific about the target or targets."

"Right Senator, we want you to know that, although we are not sure at all.... it could mean a threat to you two, now that you have become so visible. And because your platform has been so anti-crime. Some of your proposals, like the automatic death penalty for drug dealers with only one appeal, and declaring Marshall Law against drug smugglers bringing drugs into the country, are a serious threat to the international drug trade. The drug kingpins may have paid this terrorist group to eliminate you."

Sam backtracked a little, "Now mind you.... that's off the top of my head. We have absolutely no evidence of that. It's just speculation."

"I see your point though, Sam," said Governor Broadwell. "We are proposing the first and only measure to stop drug trafficking.... and they know it. If we win and get Congress to back it, we'll put an end to the drug problem in America. That's reason enough to want us dead."

"And solving the drug problem will be the beginning of an effective anti-crime movement." Senator Fleming's enthusiasm was flaring. "We know that along with the motivation of power and greed, two major factors that contribute to the commission of violent crimes against innocent people are alcohol and drugs. We can't do much about alcohol, because it has both a positive side, social acceptance, as well as a negative side."

'We already know that prohibition didn't work. Even though more young Americans have been slaughtered by alcohol than the total number of soldiers killed in all the wars since the Revolution, Americans still won't stop using it. But, illegal drugs are a different story. They have already killed too many innocent American children. If.... I should say when.... I am elected President, I'm going to put a stop to drug trafficking. Under Military Law drug dealers can be treated as enemy soldiers. If we follow our civilian legal system, we'll never stop drugs. The cost to the taxpayer is soaring out of sight. We just can't afford to baby the radical do-gooders any more."

The Senator had stepped on his political platform again without even realizing it. He had been giving so many speeches in the past six months, the words just flowed out.

"The argument the radicals use is that we must preserve the freedom of the individual under the First Amendment. I don't think the founding fathers meant for us to protect criminals who kill our children. American parents have a choice. Under our present system, which protects the rights of the vicious drug dealers, their children are slaughtered, while the drug dealers get rich. Crime is becoming so widespread that it is destroying the freedom that all Americans have. I personally would rather guarantee freedom for the good people, not the bad ones."

The Governor clapped, "Hear! Hear! Graham. You took the words right out of my mouth."

Brad sat back in silence. For the first time he could see a realistic motive. It is possible that Chaw Wi, Captain Quon, and Kuda could be the messengers of death, paid by the world-wide leaders of terrorism. There have always been megalomaniacs around, like Hitler and Mussolini in World War II, and now Quadafi, and Hussain. The technology of the 1990s has made terrorist acts by suicide bombers almost impossible to stop.

The meeting came to an end at 3:30 p.m. Sam said, "I'll keep in touch with the Governor, Senator. So he'll let you know of any urgent developments."

With the usual amenities Brad and Sam walked back down steep Fort Street and to the Arnold dock. They hopped on the 4 o'clock Catamaran heading for good old Mackinaw City.

CHAPTER 17

At 1:30 p.m. Brad was waiting at the Pellston Regional Airport, which served Petoskey, and the smaller towns in Emmet County like Harbor Springs and Mackinaw City. In the summer it was bustling with tourists on their way to Mackinac Island. The small commuter from Chicago was only a few minutes late. Billy and Alina couldn't be missed. Alina was never so stunning. Brad expected them both to look purely Hawaiian, full-length muumuu on Alina, and flowered shirt on Billy. Not so. Alina wore a snappy blue denim jumper with a pearly white long-sleeved blouse. And Billy wore neatly pressed tan slacks, with a beige short-sleeved sport shirt, button-down of course.

Billy gave Brad the brotherly hug. Alina's hug was not brotherly. It was not sisterly. She kissed him gently on both cheeks, Hawaiian style.... but then.... as if on second thought.... she gave him the more intimate Polynesian hug that sent tingles throughout his body. It was not brazen, nor presumptuous. It was a delicate admission of affection. Brad was too timid to respond with anything but an implied smile of satisfaction.

Brad said, "Mackinaw is only 20 miles, so we'll be there in a jiffy."

"Neither one of us has ever been this far north," Alina said. "I'm sure looking forward to it."

They passed the small towns of Levering and Carp Lake. As soon as they rounded the corner merging into Interstate 75, Brad blurted out in childlike excitement, "There's the bridge! There's the bridge!"

Billy laughed, "You sound like that fellow.... oh.... what's his name.... in Fantasy Island. Remember....that dere's da plane! Dere's da plane fellow."

"Tattoo.... wasn't it?" Alina ventured.

The bridge was a beautiful sight on such a clear sunny day. There were some foggy days when Brad couldn't see the bridge at all from the merge, which was about three miles out.

He drove along the main street of the historic town to show them how attractive it had become. "Ten years ago Mackinaw had a certain charm. It was old-fashioned. It was quaint and homey. The old timers liked it that way. And I did too, even though I'm not so old," he freely admitted.

"Then the town began to modernize. New motels sprung up, and the old ones got bigger. They tossed out the double beds and put in king size ones for the new generation of yuppies who.... 'want their space'. They put in colorful brick walkways, and lighted trees... just like Disney World. And now the new shopping area by the old railroad station."

Billy said, "You have to admit, it sure is an attractive town. You know how it is in Hawaii. A beautiful million dollar house on the ocean, and next door.... an old shack. It's far different around here."

"Well, you even see that in Florida.... any where there's a tropical climate," Brad opined.

After circling the town, Brad drove along Lakeside Drive to the west of the bridge, along the shore of the Straits to the log cottage. He opened the front door to the large living room, with a wide open view of the blue water of the Straits, the Mackinac Bridge, the shoreline of St. Ignace, and in the distance, Mackinac Island and the Grand Hotel. Just by chance, the 1,000 foot *Mesabi Miner* happened to be directly under the bridge, traveling west. Billy and Alina were amazed at the sight.

Billy said, "I honestly thought that there was nothing more breathtaking than the ocean views in Hawaii, but this is unbelievable. I never dreamed that there was such a view anywhere in the world."

Alina said, "Yes, it is absolutely beautiful, Brad. And how nice your cottage is. It's so homey. I know I'm going to like it here."

That made Brad feel good for some reason. He remembered the lines in the musical, Annie, after she had entered Daddy Warbucks mansion. 'I think I'm going to like it here.' These were such special friends. And he had a special feeling about Alina. He didn't know what it was.... yet. After what happened to Hui Ming, he was afraid to even think about it. He knew that his love for her was not all imaginary, because he was so devastated by her tragic death.

TUESDAY, AUGUST 13, 1996

Brad woke Billie and Alina up at 8:30 for breakfast. He proudly announced, "My Mother taught me how to make Finnish pancakes." They were different all right, they were light and puffy, and with butter and pure maple syrup, they were out of this world.

Brad had mixed his regular coffee with some pure Jamaican Blue Mountain coffee, a professor friend from Spring Arbor College had brought him. The Jamaican coffee was considered the best by some people, enough to cost $50 or $60 a pound. The Japanese loved it and imported almost the whole crop, which explained the price.

Alina was impressed with Brad's proficiency in the kitchen. It would definitely increase his market value as a husband.... a thought that didn't actually enter her mind, but would have occurred to most mainland girls.

Brad had planned several trips for them. "Let's see we'll go to the Island one day, then a drive to the Sault. We should see the Falls, and Detour, Hessel, and Cedarville. Then I'd like you to see Escanaba and Marquette..... and maybe Houghton-Hancock."

Billy said, "Why not just say the whole Upper Peninsula.... that's what you were describing. I'm surprised you didn't include Rout Reek and Rooses Rossing. Isn't that how the Finns pronounce Trout Creek and Bruce's Crossing?"

"I'm surprised you remember, Billy. We were just kids when my Dad told us that."

Alina spoke up, "I want to see Mackinac Island. Please, let's go there first. I have to see those horses and I've been wanting forever to see the romantic Grand Hotel with its 19th century glamour."

They boarded the Mackinac Express, one of the Arnold Line's catamarans, at 11:00 a.m. They left the Mackinaw City dock at 11:05, and arrived at the Island at 11:26. As they approached the harbor Brad gave his enthusiastic, and sometimes superfluous, tour guide description.

"Now to the left of the Grand is the West Bluff, with...."

Alina said, "You mean with those gorgeous mansions?"

"Yes.... and the next white mansion way over to the right of the Grand is the Governor's Summer Residence. It sounds better to the taxpayers if they don't call it a mansion. Although it doesn't really cost the taxpayers very much. It only cost $15,000 way back when, and is probably worth a million today. There.... kind of straight ahead.... is Fort Mackinac.... and to the extreme right is Mission Point Resort, where the Mackinac College used to be.

Two large Percherons pulling a shiny Grand Hotel coach, were waiting at the dock to transport eager tourists to the Hotel. Alina stopped to stroke the nose of one of the huge workhorses. Then the three friends walked across the main street, dodging not automobiles, but bicycles and horses. Next to the Chamber of Commerce, and in front of the Pub Restaurant was the small office booth for the carriage tours. Brad purchased the tickets and they boarded a carriage driven by two horses.

Right away Alina asked, "What are they, Brad?"

"I don't know everything, Alina. They must be a mix breed. I can't tell."

A few minutes later when the driver was giving his customized tour talk, he said that the horses were a mixture, unknown to him. Billy chided, "See Brad. You do know everything!"

The two sad-faced horses pulled the carriage along Huron Street, the main street with gift shops, and lots of fudge shops. They were mixing the fudge on marble slabs, so the tourists could watch with delight, after the irresistible aroma lured them inside.

"Down that way is the Chippewa Hotel, the Island House.... and further down is the historic St. Anne's Church, and Mission Point Resort," the driver rambled on. The carriage went up to Market Street, where he pointed out more attractions. "And that is the restored Robert Stuart House, where the manager of the Astor Fur Company once lived."

It then turned on Cadotte Street, up the hill toward the Grand Hotel. "What a breathtaking sight," Alina said.

Billy chided Brad, "Is that your famous.... longest porch in the world, Brad?"

Brad, who knew he was always saying.... the longest this.... and the longest that.... just said, "Yep!"

They transferred to a larger four-horse carriage. "These are Belgians," Brad proudly announced.

He knew that the large carriages had to be pulled by the heavier and stronger Belgians. This part of the tour took them to the British Landing, the route taken by the British when they captured the Fort from the Americans without a shot being fired.

Then they passed the cemeteries, one was the Post Cemetery for the soldiers and their families who lived at the Fort; one was St. Anne's Catholic Cemetery, and there was a Protestant Cemetery. Alina was more interested in the yellow Lady Slippers that the tour guide pointed out along the narrow roads.

After the carriage tour, they rented bikes at Ryba's and circled the Island. Alina had a little trouble dodging the uncontrolled teenagers, and the crazy helmeted exercise nuts, who swept around them at dangerous speeds.

After the bike ride, they stopped at the Island Book Store for Alina to buy a book with pictures of Mackinac. Then they boarded the six o'clock Catamaran for Mackinaw City.

Billy said, "Some people do have to eat once in a while.... you know Brad."

"I know.... I know.... but I wanted to take you to Darrows tonight. We're going back to the cottage so that Alina can.... well whatever women do. Then it's only a few minutes back to town. Darrows has great food... and reasonable," cheap-skate Brad had to add.

"And.... you know all of the waitresses," Alina had to speculate.

"My folks are good friends of the Darrows.... and I do know some of the waitresses. I went to school with a couple of them," Brad innocently admitted.

Of course, Brad recommended the broiled Whitefish and the Lake Perch. "Neither one is like the Mahi Mahi. They're .... well.... just different. I love Mahi, but it's more like sword-fish."

Alina had broiled, and Brad the fried Whitefish. Billy ordered the Perch.

"This.... whadayacallit.... Perch?.... is great, Brad. I like it," Billy said.

As Brad was paying the check, he reminisced, "When I was a kid, I remember going with the family.... quite a few times.... to visit my favorite Canadian Uncle. He lived at Port Stanley, over on Lake Erie. He would take me out on the pier, and sit me down, while he caught a bucketful of Perch. They were a dime a dozen then, the cheapest fish around. Now they're so scarce, they cost more than the Whitefish."

Billy grinned as he apologized, "Sorry Brad, if I had known, I would have ordered the cheaper Whitefish."

At that, the three friends burst out laughing. They re-turned to the cottage exhausted from a busy day. That night Brad treated them to the most unusual sunset.

"Even Hawaii doesn't have a sunset quite like that," Billy reluctantly admitted.

"I've never seen such unusual colors.... not only in the sky, but in the water, too. It reminds me of the water around Hanauma Bay." Alina added.

Brad said, "I know.... and the sunrises are just as spectacular. Remember.... if you have to go to the bathroom at about 6:30 in the morning, make sure you go to the front porch. You won't have to be reminded. The sky is all lit up.... pink, red, and orange. You can't miss it."

"And by the way, Billy, ol' buddy, I'm very anxious to hear about your trip to Singapore for George, but I think it can wait till tomorrow."

Brad never for a moment underestimated the seriousness of the challenge that confronted the three friends. But he knew that the diversion of the delightful Mackinac Island would temporarily delay the realities of their plight.

WEDNESDAY, AUGUST 14, 1996

The next morning Brad waited until nine o'clock before the two were up and around. They had now shaken off all effects of the jet lag. After breakfast Alina drove downtown to do some personal shopping. The two friends sat in the front porch where they could watch whatever freighters might go by.

"Now's a good time to tell me all about Singapore, Billy."

Billy started, "Let's see.... I must have flown there back on July 25th or 26th. I went to Johore Bahru and located the offices of that Raja Putra company. It was in a small industrial district. Not too large.... seemed like a small office building, and a larger building for either manufacturing.... or maybe a warehouse. I watched the buildings for three days from a rented car. The important thing is that a man in a 300 series Mercedes went into the offices two different days."

"I was staying at the Carleton Hotel in Singapore. When I returned to the hotel, I called George to check the license. He called me back and said it belonged to a man named David Bhari, and that he lives in a penthouse in Singapore. He is the president of a small electronics plant in Penang. George already knew that.... but he didn't know his name.... or where he lived. He also found that his business is called Penang Electronic Controls, Ltd. The company specializes in triggering devices. You know.... like the controls for burglar alarm systems."

"That's what George needed. Now we know he's alive and George can trace him. Remember he gave him the code name, Ikan."

"Brad, if we don't hear from George right away, I want you to call him. We need to know what has happened since we arrived. You are still in danger.... you know."

"I'll call at 11:01 tonight for sure, Billy. That way I get a cheaper rate, and it's only 5:01 in Hawaii."

Brad reached George on the phone that night. "Hello George. Billy told me about finding this Ikan fellow. He said his name is David Bhari. Is there anything else we should know?"

George said, "Yes. I found out that he has a ticket to Grand Rapids, Michigan, arriving on Thursday. He will be attending an electronics convention at the Amway Hotel."

"Do you want us to do anything.... meet him or something?"

"No Bradley. Wait until I find out more. We don't want to frighten him, and we don't want to attract any attention to him. On his return trip he is stopping at the Royal Hawaiian for two nights. He doesn't know it, but I plan on visiting him there."

"All right, George. Billy and I will wait until we hear from you."

CHAPTER 18

Thursday, August 15, 1996

David Bhari, President of Penang Electronic Controls, Ltd., landed at Chicago's O'Hare Airport at 7:27 a.m. He waited for the American commuter flight to Grand Rapids, leaving at 8:45, landing at 10:40 EDT. The International Electronics Convention was to begin on Friday at the elegant Amway Hotel. The main speaker was touted as Governor Dan Broadwell, Republican Candidate for Vice-President of the United States of America. He was scheduled to speak at the Saturday night banquet, which he had agreed to several months in advance. He seldom refused these requests, especially those with international trade potential. This time, had he realized the proximity of the Convention demands, he would not have accepted.

FRIDAY, AUGUST 16, 1996

At 4:00 p.m. on Friday the Governor's secretary received a call. "My name is David Bhari, President of Penang Electronic Controls. That is in Malaysia. I must talk personally to Governor Broadwell. It is urgent.... a matter of national concern."

"Would you hold the line, Sir. He just returned from being nominated in San Diego as the Republican candidate for the Vice-Presidency of the United States. He is very excited.... and very busy. His phone calls have been overwhelming."

"It is very urgent, Miss."

"I will try to reach the Governor for you.... if he is available."

Governor Broadwell was in his office putting the final touches on his speech. Nancy rang him, "Governor Broadwell, there is a man with a foreign accent.... probably a quack.... who thinks he has an urgent message for you. I put him on hold. Do you want me to give him some excuse?"

"Did he give his name.... and why?"

"Yes.... just a second.... he said David.... sounded like Bar-ry.... from a company in Malaysia. He said it was a matter of national concern."

"I'm really busy, so see if you can find out what he means by a national concern, Nancy."

"Sir.... Mr. Bar-ry.... are you still there?"

"Yes, yes.... I'm waiting."

"The Governor is in an important meeting right now,"

Nancy said with her fingers crossed. "It would help if I knew what you mean by national concern."

"It concerns the bombing at the Soo Locks."

"That's enough. I'll inform the Governor. One moment please."

"Governor, he said it concerns the bombing of that foreign ship at the Sault."

"Put him through, Nancy"

"Hello.... hello, is it Mister Bhari?" The Governor ventured a pronunciation. "You wanted to speak to me about the bombing?"

"Yes, Governor Broadwell, I have some information that you should know about who and why the *Singapore Soo* was bombed. It is very important that both you and Senator Fleming are apprised of this. It is not merely a regional concern. It is important to the security of your entire country."

"When can we meet?"

"I am attending the International Electronics Convention in Grand Rapids, and I see that you are the speaker at the banquet on Saturday. Could we meet before dinner?"

"Yes, I will be in the Governor's Suite. Let's meet at four. Dinner's at six, so that should give us enough time. What room are you in.... just in case?"

Mr. Bhari said, "I am in room 846."

"Would you spell out your name for me.... and what did you say your business is again?"

"My name is David Bhari, spelled B-h-a-r-i. I am the President of a company in Malaysia. We make electrical switches, and devices for triggering explosives. But I will tell you more later. I will meet you at four o'clock Saturday in the Governor's Suite. Thank you for listening to me."

Governor Broadwell said, "I should be thanking you. Goodbye for now, Mr. Bhari."

As soon as he hung up the Governor buzzed, "Nancy, get Sam Green right away."

Ten minutes later, Nancy buzzed, "Sir, I can't get through to Sam."

"Did you say it's the Governor?"

"Yes.... you know I would, Sir. The FBI office in Detroit said he's on a special undercover assignment. They are not allowed to even try to reach him. They did say that he'll be available Saturday morning.... but, only for you.

"Okay....Okay....thanks Nancy. You gave it a good try."

⌇

That evening, on the eleven o'clock news in Grand Rapids, the news anchor had a special bulletin to add to the routine local and regional news. He reported that the body of a man was just discovered, at ten o'clock on Friday night, in a wooded area, one mile north of the Wolverine Shoe Company, in Rockford, Michigan. The police reported that his neck had been broken, which was the cause of death. His face was mangled beyond recognition.

The man, approximately fifty to sixty years old, had no identification. All of his pockets had been pulled out, as if deliberately emptied. No one reported seeing any suspicious activities that would relate to the murder. The police have no further comment, except that his fingerprints were being checked. It appears that they are completely baffled.

SATURDAY, AUGUST 17, 1996

"Hello Governor, this is Sam. Sorry.... I was under-cover.... you know, the usual drug bust. I called as soon as I finished. It was a flop as usual. We risk our lives trying to stop those infernal people. But, we knew the courts would throw it out, so we had to give up. Remember.... our agent who was killed in that car last March? And for what? If we nab em.... two days later.... the dealers are right out on the streets again."

"I sure do remember that agent," the Governor commiserated.

"Look Sam, this is urgent. You remember our meeting on Mackinac Island, of course. Well, a man called David Bhari, from Malaysia, called my office, asking for me. Nancy thought he was a quack. He told her it was urgent.... and when he said it was about the *Singapore Soo* bombing, I knew it was important. He wants to meet me today at four o'clock in the Amway Hotel."

Sam was shocked, "Wait.... did he say any more?"

"I wrote it down, Sam. He said he was the President of an Electronic Controls company in Penang, Malaysia. Then he said his company made some kind of triggering controls for products such as explosives.... then he clammed up. Said he wanted to meet with me."

Sam said, "Look Dan, I didn't tell you and the Senator

everything at Mackinac, because it just wasn't.... necessary at the time. But there's always been a missing piece to our puzzle.... and he's it!"

"How's that, Sam?"

"Well.... the Singapore Girl who was murdered had a.... I guess you'd call him a kind of informer.... but, that's a long story. Anyway, he was in cahoots with this terrorist group we were telling you about. He was being forced to work with them.... kind of a blackmail deal. But, for some reason these guys over there worship these Singapore Girls.... and he worshipped Hui Ming. So he fed her information about the group. That has to be why she was killed."

The Governor said, "Wouldn't he be in trouble too?"

"I don't really know. They may not have suspected.... otherwise he might have been bumped off long before this. I'd like to be there when you meet with him, but we have to be careful."

"I was thinking the same thing, Sam. I'll meet him alone. After a few minutes, I'll explain that you want to talk to him, too."

"Good, Dan. And if he gets uptight about me, do your best to get all the info. I'll stay out, cause we don't want to scare him off."

The Governor asked, "What should I be looking for? What do you think he is going to tell me.... or us?"

"He definitely knows about some plot. Before that Singapore Girl was murdered, she managed to have someone pass on a disc to Professor Kendall. He showed us.... that is Reino Asuma and me.... you know.... he's the Chief of Police up in the Sault.... a copy of a computer disc from this Bhari guy."

"It said that these terrorist buggars have invented some kind of a new bomb, small enough to carry in a backpack and very powerful. They have made plans to place it somewhere in the United States. It said that a time and place have already been selected. So that is what we want from Bhari. I am sure that he is going to tell us the time and place."

"But, why would he call me? How did he connect me with all this? I'm just a state governor, not the FBI.... or the CIA." The Governor woefully queried from Sam.

"I am sure it's you and Senator Fleming they're after.... that's why! Because they expect you to win the election. And your policies.... you remember.... we talked about how your policies are threatening to the drug lords and to the terrorist leaders. It definitely appears that they're working together to stop your election."

The Governor said, "It seems so far fetched. We might even lose."

"Ah, but you're way ahead in the polls."

Governor Broadwell just laughed at that. "Sam, you're an optimist. Anyway, where are you calling from?"

"I'm in Lansing now. I'll see you in the Governor's Suite at 3:30 or before. I'll try to get a room nearby in case he doesn't want me to come in with you. That way we can communicate.... if necessary."

"Fine Sam, see you then."

Another agent drove Sam from Lansing to Grand Rapids straight to the Amway Hotel. He walked into the lobby and elevated to the luxurious Governor's Suite at exactly 3:30.

The Governor was alone. They shook hands, and Sam said, "I called the hotel as we were driving here. They gave me the room next door.... but just until six o'clock. That should be enough time. So I'll wait there. If he agrees to let me come in, just unlock the connecting door and knock."

Sam left through the connecting doors. He had picked up a *Grand Rapids Press* on the way up, knowing that he might have to sit for a while. His normally perspicacious eyes skimmed right over a short article on the third page about some body found north of Grand Rapids. He was too preoccupied with the anticipation of this important meeting to notice what was becoming an extremely common news report.

At a few minutes after five o'clock Governor Broadwell knocked at the connecting door. Sam opened his side and peered into the troubled face of the Governor.

He said, "He didn't come, Sam. He didn't show up. No calls. Nothing!"

"Let's go to his room. Remember the number, Dan?"

"Number 846."

"You stay here. I'll check the room right away."

One of Sam's agents joined him on the way to the lobby. Sam showed his credentials to the desk clerk and asked in an authoritative tone, "I must contact a Mr. Bhari in room 846, right now."

Checking the bill, the clerk said, "Mr. Bhari checked out at eleven this morning."

"What?" Sam spontaneously and rhetorically blurted out. "I need to see the room."

"But sir, the room has already been prepared for the next occupant. The maid would have reported anything left in the room.... and she didn't."

Sam said, "Okay, you're right. Did you check him out?"

"Yes I did. But it wasn't the same man who checked in. I assumed it was Mr. Bhari's assistant."

"Do you remember what he looked like?"

"That's why I remember them. They were both kinda oriental looking.... but the fella who checked out was big and muscular, much bigger than the man who checked in. He looked like that guy in the old movie.... you know the one.... *Of Mice and Men* with Lon Chaney.... that's what he looked like.... an oriental Lon Chaney."

"Thanks Bert. You've been a lot of help." Sam had looked at the helpful clerk's name tag.

Sam went straight to the Governor's room. "He's gone. He checked out on us, Dan. He's not going to show." Then he said as if it just dawned on him, "Wait a minute.... Dan. How could I be so stupid!"

Sam rushed back into the adjoining room, where he had waited. He went directly to the newspaper, and returned with it to the Governor's room. He looked through the pages until he located the article about the body found in the woods. This time he read it all.

"Oh my ....! He's dead, Dan!"

"Who's dead? What do you mean, Sam?"

"Listen to this from today's paper. The body of a man was discovered, late Friday night, in a wooded area, one mile north of the Wolverine Shoe Company, in Rockford, Michigan. The police reported that his neck had been broken and his face was mangled beyond recognition. Get that? His neck was broken. That's Kuda's trademark."

"Who's Kuda?"

"He's one of the leaders of the plot we told you about. Hui Ming's neck was broken, too. That's why I'm sure it was Kuda who killed that man. And that man was Bhari."

Sam read more, his voice showing more excitement. "Listen. There's more to the article. It says that the man was about five feet seven, 140 pounds, and mid-fifties. There was no identification, and no one reported seeing anything suspicious that might relate to the murder."

"And Dan, when I asked at the desk, the clerk said the man who checked out was large, very large. The guy who checked out wasn't Bhari. It was Kuda. That proves it. Bhari couldn't have checked out, because he was already dead!"

A short time later Sam left. The Governor attended the dinner and gave his speech. It wasn't easy, but politicians, especially Governors, have to be ready for all contingencies. Governor Broadwell had left this problem in good hands.... those of his friend, Sam Green. He knew Sam would pursue the matter circumspectly.

CHAPTER 19

S am called Brad on Monday and related the details of what had happened in Grand Rapids. Brad called George in Honolulu.

"Hello George. When was David Bhari supposed to arrive in Honolulu?"

"This afternoon at 2:25. I won't attempt to see him until tonight."

"Well, he may not be there." Brad told George about what happened over the weekend. "We'll be very surprised if he is on that plane."

George was noticeably disappointed. "That may have been our last chance to find out what they are planning. Now it is strictly up to you and Billy.... and of course, Sam

178

Green. I can't help you very much from here. Except.... wait, I have an idea. There is one more possibility. I have an associate.... that's a polite term for someone on our team.... over in Singapore right now on another mission. She can go to Bhari's company in Penang.... I think it is less than 200 miles away.... and find out more about that triggering device. That may be the key to Bhari's involvement.... and could explain why he was so important to Chaw Wi and Kuda."

"That sounds like a good idea. And we'll do all we can over here to stop them. I'll keep you informed, George. Call me or Sam as soon as you have any information from Penang."

〜〜〜

"Well, Billy and Alina. There's nothing we can possibly do about this mess right now, so Sam said to have a good time and forget all about it for a while."

Alina said, "I would like to see the Tahquamenon Falls, Brad. Is it very far?"

"Heavens no, it's only about 80 miles or so. We can spend a day there, but I want to spend a day at the Soo Locks first."

"Are they back in operation?" Alina asked.

Brad said, "Yes, they were back in operation in the middle of July."

Brad called Reino at the Sault. "Allo Reino. How've ya bin? Ave ya bin ta Rout Reek lately?

"Cut the Finglish, Brad. I know it's you."

Brad tried again, "Naw it ain't, it's yer Uncle Toivo. Cain't ya rekonize an ol' Finn when ya hear one?"

Reino laughed, "Uncle Toivo's dead, Brad. You goofed on that one."

"Hi Reino. I just can't fool you. How about some company? I told you that Billy and Alina were coming. They want to see the Sault tomorrow. How about lunch?"

Reino said, "Let's see.... Tuesday.... looks all clear. I'll make a reservation at the Freighter's. Would you like me to bring Susan.... for Alina's sake, that is?"

"Great. Maybe Susan could drive Alina around town.... so we could talk. And you and Billy and I do need to talk. You know what I mean? A lot has happened since we last saw each other."

"I sure do. I'll make sure that Susan gets the hint."

TUESDAY, AUGUST 20, 1996

On Tuesday morning Billy and Alina were on their way to Sault Ste. Marie with Brad, in his 1993 blue Buick LeSabre.

"It's a little scary up here, I'm glad you're driving," Alina said as they approached the center of the Mackinac Bridge. Brad drove them through the main street in St. Ignace.

"Right there," Brad said. "That's where the Christmas trees are lined up. They mark the safest path straight across to Mackinac Island. The snowmobilers need the trees, especially when the weather is stormy."

"That would scare me to death," Billy said. "Don't they ever fall through the ice?"

"Occasionally," Brad answered rather matter-of-factly.

Alina said, "This is a nice town. I thought Hawaii had so much water. But there seems to be water everywhere, here in Michigan."

They arrived at the first exit to Sault Ste. Marie fifty minutes later. Reino had arranged for lunch at the Freighters Restaurant in the Ojibway Hotel, overlooking the Locks, at noon. Reino and Susan were waiting at the table when they arrived. Susan and Alina made instant friends. Susan had a million questions to ask about Hawaii, and Alina had just as many about the Upper Peninsula. The men were ignored, but had plenty to talk about.

After lunch Reino said to Alina, "Susan will take you for a little tour of the town, if you would like. Won't you Susan?"

Susan gave him a funny look, and said, "Of course, I will."

"Meet us back at my office in two hours. Okay, Susan?" Susan just nodded.

At his office Reino said, "I knew you couldn't tell me what's been happening with a newswoman present. Susan is always cooperative with me, but some news is irresistible. And as we well know, this is a matter of life and death."

"And this could be a matter of not just national, but worldwide security," Billy added.

Brad told Reino all that had happened since they last talked. "Sam and I are convinced that they are after the Republican candidates. Sam has informed the Secret Service that there is the possibility of a threat to their lives.

But, without anything but a hunch, they have to follow normal procedures. And Sam won't reveal any details to anyone else, until we have something more definite."

Two hours and five minutes later, Susan and Alina appeared at Reino's office door. Alina said, "Susan is a wonderful tour guide, Brad. We went all around the downtown area. We didn't go inside, but I saw the Valley Camp Museum Ship and the Tower of History. Then we drove out to see the university campus. Did you know that the campus was originally a fort? Fort Brady. Wasn't that the name, Susan?"

"Yes, I believe the Fort was built back around the time of World War I. Then much later, Michigan Tech used some of the old buildings for a two year campus. Isn't that about right, Reino?"

Reino said, "That's pretty close, Susan, except that technically there was no World War I."

Susan yiped with chagrin, "What do you mean there was no World War I? Of course there was a World War I."

"Well.... I said technically. If it were possible to talk to a soldier killed in the war of 1914 to 1918, and ask him the name of the war he fought in.... you would hear any one of several names, but not World War I."

"There couldn't be a war called World War I until November of 1939, when World War II started. It was called the Great War, the War in Europe, even the Great World War, but not World War I. People just assume that everything we read and hear is true, without verifying it. One advantage of being an investigative police officer is a suspicious, and an inquisitive mind."

Brad said, "You convinced me Reino. And I thought you were just a backwoods Yupanite. By the way, that reminds me. I didn't tell you before this, because it wasn't definite. The Business School at Lake Superior State University has offered me a position starting in January. I'm leaving Michigan State. Back in the days when the Accounting Department was ranked sixth in the nation.... way ahead of Michigan.... it was enjoyable to teach there. Now sports programs, not academic programs, control the priorities, and second-rate administrators, not the faculty, run the university. My responsibility is to profess my scholarly knowledge. Professors don't teach.... they profess. And that's the problem right there."

Susan said, "What do you mean.... professors don't teach?"

Brad inadvertently changed to his classroom, authoritative tone, "We're scholars, not teachers. I have a Ph.D..... but I have no teaching certificate authorizing me to teach high school, or even grade school. I'm not even qualified to teach kindergarten."

"College students learn from the superior knowledge conveyed to them by the professor, not by the teaching skills of the professor. Virtually all lawyers, medical doctors, accountants, teachers, engineers, natural and social scientists, and even Ph.D.s have learned from professors. They must be legitimized by professors before they can practice their profession."

Susan chided Brad, "Is that your fifty minute lecture, Professor?"

Brad facetiously replied, "I've got five minutes left, Susan."

He went on, oblivious to how automatically he shifted back to his pedagogical gear. "Nothing at the university should take precedence over the classroom experience. That's how the principle of autonomy in the classroom developed. As long as the professor is honest, ethical, and follows the rules of conduct and behavior established by the faculty, the professor has autonomy in the classroom."

"The practice of student evaluations of university professors is absurd. Allowing student evaluations to be used as a basis for official faculty rank, salary, and tenure decisions recognizes only teaching skill, not superior expertise and knowledge of subject matter."

Billy's intellectual prowess was aroused, "That's a fine theoretical lecture, my friend, but it's anachronistic."

Reino chimed in, "Hey scholars.... not such big words. Try KISS....keep it simple, stupid.... at least for me. What the heck is.... ana-kron-stick.... or however you say it?"

Billy said, "Brad is back in the 50s and 60s.... before respect for the faculty was abolished, and before grade inflation. Now anyone who can walk into class gets an A. Those who can just stagger in, after last night's beer party, get a B. When students control the tenure and promotion process, they control the grades. It's a form of blackmail. The professor who goes out drinking with the students, who dresses like a bum, and gives all As and Bs, gets the highest student evaluations."

"Hear, hear, Billy thinks like me.... in some things.... that is," Brad said.

Billy loved the center stage, "Forgive my choice of words again, Reino, but in today's society egalitarianism prevails."

Something that sounded like 'holy cats' was barely audible from Reino.

Billy went on, "By reducing everyone to the same level, as the egalitarians want, professors are just buddies. Calling everyone.... parents, teachers, clergy.... by their first name reduces them to a child's level. There are no authority figures anymore. Some university professor wrote an article recently saying that the major cause of teenage crime in America was the absence of authority figures to provide discipline."

Alina finally put her two cents into the conversation. "And what were we talking about before this intellectual digression into our iconoclastic society..... if I may use one of my own esoteric words. Sorry, Captain Asuma! Oh.... I hope I pronounced your name correctly?"

Reino responded, "Oh.... you did.... but, I'm not really a captain. I'm a Chief of Police. But I don't want you to call me Chief. I want you to call me Reino. Yes.... please call me Reino."

Susan said, "I think Brad.... Dr. Kendall, that is," pulling one of her little digs, "was telling us that he will be teach.... sorry.... professing, at LSSU this fall. You have forgotten.... haven't you.... that we are the Hockey champs?"

Brad rationalized a bit, "Well that's different. Hockey doesn't get the media attention that football and basketball get. It's more regional. And don't get me wrong. Sports are good for young people. There's nothing better.... at a truly amateur level. But money talks. In the professional sports, there are few, if any, bona fide athletes."

"The stars of the major sports are not real people; they are products. Everything they do is governed by profitability of the product line. If fighting on the basketball court improves profits, they fight. If acting like an idiot.... throwing the football down, and jumping up and down, gets more viewers.... that's what they do. Can you imagine true athletes like Joe Louis, or Ted Williams acting so stupid?"

"Back to the question. Yes, Lake Superior State still seems to have an atmosphere of academic respectability. I need it in order to function effectively as a professor."

A few minutes later, at 4:15 p.m., they all walked over to the Soo Locks. Reino explained the models of the four locks in the Welcome Station to Alina and Billy. Alina, pointing to a chalkboard, asked the lady at the counter, "Are those the ships coming in today?"

"Yes, the *Algowood* is due in the MacArthur Lock in a few minutes. Then the *Darya Ma* is due at 4:45."

Billy was curious, "*Darya Ma*, what a strange name for a ship. Where is it from?"

The lady started looking through a book named, *Know Your Ships*. "There's a lot of strange names. Here it is.... I found it. It is registered in Hong Kong."

They all went outside by the sightseeing tower, next to the MacArthur Lock. Alina said, "I don't see any sign of the damage, Captain Asuma.... excuse me, I meant to say Reino."

Alina had looked up coquettishly into Reino's face with her twinkling brown eyes and captivating smile as she spoke. The busy Finlander had paid no attention to her charm, when all of a sudden it struck him like a bolt of lightning.

Reino just stared at her for a few seconds and then stammered. "About the damage.... they fixed it up pretty good, I would say. There are still some patched areas on the other side of the visitor's tower. And you can't see some of the underwater repairs that are still temporary."

From that moment on, Susan noticed that Reino was very attentive to Alina. He opened doors for her, and was ready and willing to answer her every question. Brad noticed it too. He had reacted the same way when he first met Hui Ming. Any virile unattached man would find it difficult to ignore Alina. Her charm was exuding into Reino's masculine yearnings.

The hibernation of Susan's affection for Reino, and the obscurity of Brad's feelings for Alina came to an abrupt end. They both had a twinge of real jealousy.

At the next doorway they encountered, Susan stood waiting. She always opened doors for herself when she was with Reino. This time she would let Reino do it. He was right next to her. Billy rushed around Reino to open it for her. Reino was too busy talking to Alina. He was pointing at the next ship entering the locks.

After Brad, Billy and Alina took off for Mackinaw City, Reino drove Susan home. He said, "That was a lot of fun today, wasn't it Susan? That Billy and Alina are a treat to have around, aren't they?"

Susan gave him a look of disgust. "Yes Reino, they were very nice. That Alina is very sweet. You can't help but like her. And she's beautiful, too."

"Oh.... I hardly noticed."

"Yes, I noticed that you hardly noticed!"

Reino looked puzzled at that statement. Then, as he pulled up in front of her apartment, he said, "You know, Susan.... I wish you'd let me open doors for you. I like to open the door for a lady. And I'd like you to be more like a lady friend.... instead of being like a buddy friend."

Although a mere man could never comprehend the complexities of love, Susan fully understood that Alina had served as a catalyst to stir up Reino's affection for her.

When Susan stepped out of the car, she leaned over and gave Reino a soft kiss on the cheek and said, "I'm your lady friend, Reino, and from now on.... you open all my doors!"

Brad drove through Cedarville, and then Hessel so he could show Alina and Billy some of the old Chris Craft cabin cruisers still around after the Les Cheneaux Islands Antique Wooden Boat Show that was held on August 10th. They drove back over the Mackinac Bridge to Mackinaw City.

"I'm hungry," Billy declared.

"You're always hungry," his sister asserted.

"But, we haven't eaten since noon.... and it's almost seven o'clock. Where do they have good pizzas, Brad?"

Brad said, "Mama Mia's, Pizza Palace, Squealy's.... and there's a Mancino's. They all have good pizzas. We can order a pizza and take it home, if you'd like."

Billy and Alina agreed. They were both worn out from the driving, and the busy day at the Sault. They were not used to long drives. A complete drive around Oahu is only 90 miles.

Before falling off to sleep that night, Brad said, "If that wore you out today, wait until Thursday, when we drive to Escanaba and Marquette. That'll be like driving around the Big Island twice.... and more."

Instead of an audible response, he heard something that sounded like moans or groans..... and then silence, from the other two bedrooms.

THURSDAY, AUGUST 22, 1996

Brad woke Alina and Billy up to a beautiful sunny day. They drove over the majestic Mackinac Bridge after a scrumptious breakfast of gourmet pancakes at Audie's Restaurant. At the middle of the bridge Brad said, "Look Alina, you can see for miles today."

Alina uncovered her eyes, took a quick glance, saw the 200 foot drop to the water, quickly covered her eyes again, and said, "I see, I see.... it's breathtaking." She put one hand on her stomach, muttered something under her breath that, if it were audible, would sound like, "Why is it always right after breakfast?"

Then they drove along the north shore of Lake Michigan to Cut River Bridge. Brad stopped to show them the panoramic view, "See Hawaii doesn't have all the beauty."

They went through Manistique, Rapid River, and finally Escanaba. Brad showed them the beautiful Little Bay de

Noc. He stopped briefly to say hello to his mother's Finnish sisters, Dorothy and Ruth. Alina wondered why Brad called them Aunt Dorty and Aunt Ruuty. His aunts told Alina and Billy the story of the Finnish Saint Urho, who chased all the grasshoppers out of the saunas in Finland. After they left, Brad simply said, "Don't believe anything you heard from my Finnish aunts."

From there Brad drove up to Marquette on Lake Superior. They stayed overnight in a motel along Marquette Bay. The next day, on Friday, Brad drove them up to Big Bay, just north of Marquette.

"This is where Anatomy of a Murder was filmed. The actual murder took place over there in a trailer park."

Back in Marquette, he said, "That's where Jimmy Stewart's law office was.... and there's the Court House... right in that old building."

They had lunch with a professor friend of Brad's, and his wife, from Northern Michigan University. He called them Jim and Lois. After a lot of tall stories, Brad said to Billy and Alina, "He's another Finn. Maybe you better not believe him either. There must be some Finns who don't have a sense of humor, but they're hard to find."

They drove home along M-28 through Munising, along the Seney stretch, 22 miles of perfectly straight highway, on to Newberry, and back to Mackinaw City.

Exhausted, Billy asked, "How far did we drive, Brad?"

"Well, it's 140 miles to Escanaba, another 60 to Marquette, and 175 back from Marquette to the bridge. Then if we add the round trip from Marquette to Big Bay, we drove a total of about 450 miles."

Alina was pooped, to put it indelicately, but explicitly. That night she fell asleep early without a word. Billy wasn't good company either. They were not used to this kind of driving.

CHAPTER 20

Monday, August 26, 1996

Alina's first words that morning were, "Let's have breakfast in St. Ignace, please."

This time, tucked in the back seat of Brad's Buick, she covered her eyes as they crossed over the 8,600 foot suspended portion of the Mackinac Bridge. The rest of the five mile bridge didn't bother her, but the length between the two anchorage piers, No. 17 and No. 22, was nearly 1,000 feet longer than the suspended span of the Golden Gate Bridge. Enough to take the breath away from anyone squeamish about heights.

At the Big Boy, Brad ordered, before 11:00 a.m., his favorite $1.99, mini-breakfast, consisting of one egg, two pieces of bacon, and cheese toast, designed especially for cheapskates like Brad. Out of politeness, Billy and Alina ordered one of the mini-specials too.

Billy read the tourist brochure, "It says that Tahquamenon Falls is the second largest falls east of the Mississippi. What are they trying to say, Brad?"

Brad answered, glad that he once had to teach.... profess, that is.... a course in Economic Geography.

"Well Niagara Falls is obviously the largest falls, with an over 150 foot drop.... so on this side of the Mississippi, Tahquamenon, with about a fifty foot drop, is next largest. And Niagara is massive, but not the highest in America. Angel Falls in South America, I think it's in Venezuela, is ten.... maybe twenty times higher than Niagara.

From the bridge at St. Ignace, Brad drove seven miles up the thruway, I-75, to Highway 123, passing through Trout Lake. They reached Paradise, the nearest town to the Falls, at noon.

Paradise was a picturesque little town located on Lake Superior's Whitefish Bay. Only a dozen or so miles north was Whitefish Point, the most dangerous waters on earth, if measured by shipwrecks. From the wreck of the schooner, *Invincible*, in 1816, to the *Edmund Fitzgerald*, in 1975, the violent raging storms have outsmarted the most erudite, and perhaps too courageous, sea captains for more than a century and a half. From Paradise, Brad drove ten miles to the Lower Tahquamenon Falls.

He said, "My professor friends at CMU.... you've heard me talk about Phil and Art.... anyway, they told me that you can start at either end, because you have to walk back to get the car, anyway. So we can start here, walk to the Upper Falls, rest for a while, and then return to the Lower Falls."

That was all Alina needed. "What is the walk like, Brad?"

"I have to admit, I have never walked it before. My friend said it was pretty rugged, though."

"That settles it," Alina triumphantly said, "I'll stay here, in the park, and then drive the car to meet you at the Upper Falls. That way you two won't have to walk back."

She thought a minute, "And while you're gone, I'll be able to see the Lower Falls here.... if I want to. Then, if I'm not too tired, I'll be able to see the Upper Falls when I drive there to pick you up. Aren't they the big ones, Brad, and doesn't that make more sense?"

Billy gave her a brotherly response, "Well only if you are determined not to walk the four miles, Alina. She is kind of lazy, Brad. And after all that work dolling herself up to look spiffy for you, she doesn't want to mess it up."

Alina swatted brother Billy on the arm, "Billy, you beast. How could you be so.... so nasty!"

Brad said, "Alina is right.... oh, I didn't mean about the beast, Billy.... I mean about the walk. If that's what you prefer, Alina.... I can understand. We will probably take at least two hours to reach the Upper Falls. It's mostly uphill. And you're right.... they are the big ones. Right here in the park is a good place to wait. Then in about two hours.... drive to the Upper Falls. We'll meet you in the parking lot. There must be some kind of a Welcome Center for visitors there.... they have to have bathrooms somewhere.

If you're not in the car, we'll look for you at the Welcome Center."

Billy and Brad started their four mile trek to the Upper Falls, reaching the site in a little less than two hours. They climbed down to the lookout area, where they stopped to admire the beauty of the clear blue water rushing over the top, 50,000 gallons per second, splashing down 50 feet to the rocks below.

Brad said, "I know it takes a lot of climbing, but I think that Alina would like to see this. You stay here and enjoy the view, Billy, while I go and find her. We should be back in about a half hour. Why don't you climb to the upper level and meet me, just in case she doesn't want to come."

It took Brad about fifteen minutes to reach the parking lot. It had started to sprinkle lightly. The tourists had all scattered to the building, or to their cars. Brad spotted his car way over in a corner of the lot. When he arrived there, the door was open and the motor was running. Alina's purse strap was dangling over the side of the front seat.

Brad called out for her, and looked all around the car. Then he looked around the parking lot. The Welcome Center was not close by. Besides, he thought.... she would never leave the car running, or leave her purse, to go to the rest rooms. Suspecting foul play, he turned the motor off, locked the door, and took the key.

He tried to hurry back to where he had left Billy. The uphill part of the climb was exhausting. When he first saw Billy he shouted, "Billy, hurry.... It's Alina. Something's wrong.... hurry."

He stopped to catch his breath. "She wasn't there.... the car is in the lot.... the motor was running, but Alina wasn't in it. I'm worried."

"Maybe she had to go to the bathroom in a hurry," Billy said, but didn't even convince himself.

Brad said, "If anything happens to Alina I'll never forgive myself."

Billy said, "Look.... over there.... in the woods. That big fellow."

The light rain made it difficult to see clearly. It looked like a hulk of a man dragging something toward the river above the Falls. Billy and Brad ran toward the man. As he reached the river bank, they clearly saw Alina. The big man had his arm around her neck, dragging her along the ground. Brad caught up to them. Alina screamed, "He wants you, Brad.... not me.... run."

Billy had come from behind and threw himself into the giant of a man. His relatively lightweight body merely bounced off, and he fell to the wet ground. When Brad came close enough, the man threw Alina roughly to the ground, and grabbed him around the neck.

Brad anticipated the hold and thrust his arm upward, between the monster's arm and his own neck. Just as the pressure on his arm and neck was becoming unbearable, Billy grabbed a rock and struck the man on the elbow. It was just enough to stop the assailant from snapping Brad's neck.

In a rage, the man lifted Brad off the ground, into the air above his head, and threw him into the swirling waters, just ten yards upstream from the Falls. Billy got up and tried to tackle the man again, but he bounced off and fell to the ground once more. The monster of a man reached down to pick Billy up, apparently to throw him in too, when several hikers appeared. They had been sheltering themselves from the drizzle. The sun had just emerged, and the light rain had stopped completely. Seeing the commotion, they rushed over to help. The mysterious man ran into the woods in the direction of the parking lot, and disappeared.

Brad was a strong swimmer, but he couldn't make any headway upstream. He was drawn slowly, but inexorably toward the 50 foot drop over the Falls. He wasn't quite sure of the consequences of such a fall, but he wasn't anxious to personally find out. About seven or eight feet before the drop, a tree branch jutted out from the bank. Brad concentrated all his strength to swim to the branch, and was able to grab it before reaching the plunging waters over the Falls.

Billy raced to the tree and crawled out as far as he could. He stretched out, while two of the tourists held on to his legs, to reach Brad's hands. They managed to pull him to safety on the bank. After the ordeal, Billy and Brad had to lie on the wet ground for several minutes to catch their breath.

The tourists, there were three men and three women of college age, seemed anxious to leave, once they were assured that everyone was safe. Alina thanked them for helping. Then, after a few more minutes of catching their breath, Brad, Billy, and Alina walked backed to the car.

From the Upper Falls, Brad drove down toward

Newberry, then over to Highway 123, and south toward the Straits.

Brad said, "Thanks again for pulling me out, Billy. I don't want to think about what would happen if I went over those falls."

"You'd do the same for me, Brad."

"Do you think it was Kuda, Brad?" Alina asked, anticipating the answer.

"I most certainly do," Brad said. "Don't you, Billy?"

"Who else could it be! Who else breaks necks! He had you in his arm lock.... and Alina, too. But why didn't he.... I'm sorry to bring this up, Alina.... because I'm so thankful that he didn't.... but why did he let you go? He could easily have.... you know.... what he does best.... or worst.... you know what I mean, don't you, Brad?"

Alina answered, "I know why. He wanted Brad to follow him. He could have easily hauled me off to the woods and killed me. But he purposely let you two see him by the Falls. He didn't actually talk, but he kept mumbling. I could tell that he wanted Brad somehow. He deliberately dropped me to grab Brad. He probably would have....oh dear....I hate to talk about it....or even think about it. He would have done it if you hadn't bumped into him when you did, Billy."

"That's a laugh.... I bounced right off him. It was like trying to knock a tree down."

Brad said, "Yes.... but, Billy.... it stalled him just enough so he had to grab me. It probably stopped him from breaki.... I mean hurting Alina. And when you hit him with that rock.... why.... you saved me there too Billy."

Back at the cottage in Mackinaw City, Brad said, "How about a sauna? My dad had the kit shipped right from Finland, rocks and everything."

The sauna was a small building, a few steps from the cottage. He turned on the electric unit that heated the rocks. It was ready in less than an hour. Like most real Finns, Brad didn't like wearing a bathing suit, so the two men went first, and then Alina went in later.

Brad had forgotten to give Alina a towel, so he took one out to her. He knocked on the door, which had a twelve inch wide glass strip down the middle. It allowed the people in the sauna to watch the ships go by on the Straits as they were sitting on the benches.

"Alina, here's your towel."

Alina opened the door wide, in full view. Her provocative tanned body was enough to cause an earthquake in the involuntary masculine responses to such an unexpected gift of feminine delicacies. Then she very slowly reached out her hand for the towel, allowing Brad to get a nice long look at her indescribable physical attributes that make women so much more delightful to look at than men.

"Oh I'm sorry," she coyly said as she pretended to be embarrassed.

Brad wanted to say, "Well I'm not." But he didn't. He just smiled at her, managed to turn around, flustered, mumbling something, and stumbled back to the cottage.

It reminded him of the time that he was a young boy. His father had a house built in Ann Arbor that had an attached room with an indoor swimming pool, a sauna, and a bathroom at one end. One day two businessmen from Finland were in town. The owner of the business they called on was a friend of Brad's father. He asked if the two Finns, who spoke only a little English, could come over and have a sauna. Brad's father was delighted and invited them for lunch and sauna.

When the Finnish men were in the sauna, Brad's mother walked into the poolroom with a tray of food. Both men, stark naked, walked out of the sauna to take the tray from her. She squealed with embarrassment, turned around, and handed the tray to her husband. Finns just don't wear bathing suits in the sauna.

But this was different. Both Brad and Alina knew that she could have stuck her arm out the sauna door for the towel. Except for the short spurt of jealousy over Reino's attentiveness to Alina, Brad had reclined right back into his polite, platonic attitude toward her. Alina thought that a little shock treatment might help. It did.... for the moment. Brad's subconscious desire for her suddenly became a burning desire when he saw her standing there in the.... , but that couldn't be.

Alina's charm and beauty emanated from within. Brad was never attracted to women for purely sexual reasons. That was for shallow, low class people, like movie and television producers.... and novelists who would sell their soul to the devil for a best seller.... in his opinion. Perhaps, only in his opinion, according to what people read.

He recently started to read a national bestseller that had won a Pulitzer Prize. By page three, the woman author had already used the four-letter "F" word. He stopped reading it, figuring that if gutter language is now necessary to win the Pulitzer, he could do without. Then he tried best-selling novels by the major authors, both men and women. But they used so much irrelevant pornography and offensive language he couldn't finish.

After the sauna, Alina came in without saying a word. She gave Brad a saucy little smile and went into the bedroom to dress. The three friends had a late dinner at Audie's Restaurant, then returned to the cottage to recapitulate the nasty episode at Tahquamenon Falls.

Brad stated, "We have to contact both George in Honolulu, and Sam Green. He should be in either Detroit or Lansing. But first, we have to try to figure out what's going on in Kuda's and this Chaw Wi guy's minds. For some reason, they are determined to kill all four of the people at that meeting in Singapore."

Billy said, "Maybe George left a message on your machine?"

Brad replied, "No, he will not leave a message. He's very careful about that. And he may have tried to call us when we were gone. I'll give him a call right away."

"Hello George, this is Brad. We were gone off and on for a few days."

George said, "I know, I tried to call twice in the last two or three days. I heard from our associate in Singapore. She went to Penang and had a good reception from the Plant Manager. He said that David Bhari was still in the United States, but he had no word from him in over a week. He thought that was strange. I did not tell the associate what we know must have happened to Bhari."

Brad said, "It's only an assumption, anyway. And we have to be careful not to be linked to any of Kuda's business. By the way, he tried to kill me again."

George was shocked, "What, how.... what happened?"

Brad said, "He seemed to want me, but not Alina or Billy. I assume it was Kuda. He was about six feet tall, husky, and muscular. But I can't understand why he didn't look more Asian. He had what I could only call.... a nondescript face. Anyway.... he had a vice grip around my neck. He had a chance to kill Alina, but waited for me to come instead. He threw me into a waterfall.... and.... well I'll give you the details later. Right now I want to know about Penang."

"I'm just thankful that you're alive Bradley. We must stop these megalomaniacs before they strike again. The Plant Manager in Penang would not give our associate the information we needed, so she called me."

"I had to fly there myself. After I explained that Bhari was most certainly murdered by Chaw Wi and Kuda, the Plant Manager said he knew exactly what it was all about. Bhari had told him and no one else."

George stopped, "Just a minute, Bradley, I need to look for something. Here it is. The Manager said that they had developed a new triggering mechanism just for Raja Putra, Ltd. He said it was simple, but so different that no bomb expert would be able to figure it out in time. He gave me the wiring diagram to defuse the device. Do you have your fax turned on, Bradley? I wouldn't normally send a fax.... but this is an emergency."

"Just a minute." Bradley turned on his computer and said, "Okay, it'll be ready when we hang up."

George said, "I'll send you the diagram right away. You'll need a small pair of wire clippers and pliers. Call me as soon as you have any new information."

"I will, George, goodbye for now."

"Wait, before you hang up. I have one more important fact. The *Kapitan Malaga* left Singapore on July 27th. It will arrive at Chicago on August 29th. It may be the key to where Kuda will be."

"When is it due to pass the Mackinac Bridge on the way back from Chicago?"

George said, "I don't know, but I'll try to find out."

"Okay, thank you, George."

Brad was going to tell Billy and Alina about the conversation, but they were too tired to absorb it. Brad decided to wait until morning.

The next morning he called Sam. Sam said that he would be flying into Chippewa County Airport tomorrow, on Wednesday. The FBI would arrange for a car, and he would drive to Mackinaw City to meet with them. He had to be on hand for Governor Broadwell's meetings on Mackinac Island.

Brad said, "We have a lot to discuss.... I guarantee you, Sam. Someone tried to kill me again, and maybe Billy and Alina too. But there's too much to say.... so I'll tell you about it tomorrow."

CHAPTER 21

G overnor Broadwell had made early reservations at the Grand Hotel, and at Mission Point Resort for several Republican Governors who brought their families along for a vacation. The official strategy meetings for the 31 governors and other party leaders would begin on Friday, August 30th. The theme of the meetings was to coordinate the strategy established at the 1995 meetings on Mackinac Island, and to adapt to any major changes in the political scene since then.

This time they planned an even more organized, concentrated attack on crime, based on the shocking statistics on violence by teenagers. Governor Broadwell had invited Professor Clayton Hopping who had recently published an article entitled: "The Activities That Cause Crime in America." He was a realist when it came to crime. He predicted an upcoming teenage crime wave exceeding our wildest fears.

WEDNESDAY, AUGUST 28, 1996

Sam flew into Chippewa County Airport, where a 1995 Pontiac Bonneville sedan was reserved for him. He drove to St. Ignace and across the Mackinac Bridge to the cottage.

"It's easy to find." Brad had said on the phone, "Drive along Lakeside Drive about a half mile until you come to a log cottage with the sign, The Kendall's."

Sam drove off the first bridge exit, past the Shell gas station, turned right in front of Darrow's Restaurant, toward the Fort, and then turned left on the short street that led to Lakeside Drive.

"Howdy Sam," Brad greeted him. "Have you ever met Billy and Alina?"

Sticking out his hand, Sam said, "No, but I've heard a lot of good things about both of you."

What he thought was, that Brad hadn't said enough of the good things.... the feminine charm, that is.... about Alina. But that was typical of Brad.

After they all sat down around the long Rittenhouse dining table, Sam said, "Brad mentioned that someone tried to kill him.... or was it all of you?"

Alina and Billy took turns explaining what happened. Then Sam said, "Now is the time for us to.... let us say.... figure out, and anticipate, what is being planned by these guys, Chaw Wi Chan, Kuda, and Captain Quon. First, we should figure out why David Bhari wanted to meet with Governor Broadwell."

Brad said, "It seems logical that the Governor might be the target of Bhari's former associates, Chaw Wi, and company."

Billy added, "It's even more likely that both Senator Fleming and Governor Broadwell are the targets because they are running together."

"I agree," Alina said. "And it also seems logical that the attack will take place in this area. I think it will be either Mackinac Island.... or the Mackinac Bridge."

"Absolutely," Brad said, "I think it will be the Mackinac Bridge because it would be so devastating. They would really get the attention of the world. The bombing of the Soo Locks was a kind of training ground for them to.... to practice for this big one."

Sam scowled, "That creates a serious problem. If I go to my superiors and tell them that a man named Chaw Wi Chan is planning to blow up the Mackinac Bridge, they would think I'm crazy. We don't have enough tangible evidence to go on."

"If I release our suspicions to the press, Kuda and his gang would probably back down. And then.... the news would make a fool out of me, and the FBI. You saw what they did to the FBI because of Waco. My superiors are sensitive. They can't make any foolish mistakes. They will insist that the usual protection for presidential candidates is adequate."

Billy said, "And if we tried to explain our theory publicly, we could create some international problems, too. We seem to have no choice. We must solve it ourselves."

Sam said, "If you all agree, and we need Reino here too, I think we can work as a team to stop whatever plan they have. And if we're all crazy, and there is no threat to the Governor and the Senator, then nobody will know the difference. We'll keep the whole thing quiet and never say a word to anyone else about our suspicions. How does that sound?"

After they all agreed, Brad called Reino. He agreed to be there, in Mackinaw City, on Sunday, and stay until Monday afternoon, after the Bridge Walk was finished.

Sam said, "Because of the Governor's meetings, I'll have a lot to do from now until Labor Day. Some of the Governors came early with their families to enjoy Mackinac Island. I'm in charge of routine protective measures. Call me at the Mackinac Island Police Station.... anytime."

Then Sam displayed his brand of humor, "You know.... that's the only one in America that uses bicycles instead of police cars."

THURSDAY, AUGUST 29, 1996

The *Kapitan Malaga* arrived in Chicago on Thursday, August 29th. The cargo of Asian-manufactured clothing was being unloaded. On Thursday afternoon, a tall muscular Asian man deplaned at O'Hare Airport and took a taxi to the docks. He walked up the gangplank to the deck of the *Kapitan Malaga*.

Captain Quon said, "Mr. Kuda, I haven't heard anything from you since Singapore."

"No one has, my dear Captain. I make sure that no one can trace me when I am working. If not, I would never have reached the age of .... that is.... I would not be here today."

Konji Kuda said, "Where is my friend, Chaw Wi?"

"He said he was going to Jimmy Wong's. I wonder if there still is a Jimmy Wong's? I think it is his way of not telling me where he is actually going. Just like you.... my dear Mr. Kuda."

Chaw Wi returned to the ship at nine o'clock that evening. "Konji, you have accomplished much since our last meeting. I must compliment you for your.... shall we say.... elimination of obstacles to the fulfillment of our special assignment. But, how did you know that our friend Bhari had plans to betray us?"

Kuda said, "I followed him closely back in Malaysia and Singapore. He went to the cemetery where that Singapore Girl was buried, every day. That convinced me that his relationship with that girl was more than casual. He could be trusted no more. His trip to that convention in Michigan was convenient.... for me.... that is.... not for our lamented Mr. Bhari."

Chaw Wi said, "Yes, of course. You were to meet us here anyway. It was indeed, convenient."

Kuda did not mention anything about a visit to the Tahquamenon Falls in the Upper Peninsula. It wasn't his style to talk about unsuccessful missions, unless it was absolutely necessary. He saw no advantage in telling Chaw Wi or Captain Quon about this forgettable one, because he was not sure of the outcome of his attempt to kill Professor Kendall.

Chaw Wi said, "That means you now have only one more.... shall we say.... obstacle to remove. Is that not so, my stalwart friend?"

"Yes, you are correct, Chaw Wi. Perhaps I shall have an opportunity very soon. What are the plans?"

Chaw Wi outlined the ominous plan to Captain Quon and to Kuda. "Konji, you will drive a rented automobile.... it is already on the docks.... to Interstate 94. It is a black Toyota Camry.... here is the key and license number. Drive all the way to Mt. Clemens, Michigan. Get off on Highway 29 and drive to Algonac. Spend a day or two.... whatever is necessary.... to locate a place for your return to the ship. You may find that either Walpole or Harsen's Island, or Robert's Landing is the best place."

"Then drive up Interstate 75 to Mackinaw City. I made a reservation for you under another name. You must be there on Sunday, by six o'clock, to avoid using a credit card. Your new credentials, and your makeup bag are in the trunk of the car, along with the backpack. It is quite heavy, naturally."

Chaw Wi stopped for a few minutes to pour what looked like green tea. "The *Kapitan Malaga* will pass under the Mackinac Bridge precisely one half hour before the Bridge Walk begins. You will perform your mission and return to your automobile. You must leave the vehicle at the motel. It was carefully selected to be far enough away from the bridge to avoid being trapped by tourist traffic."

"We both know," deliberately omitting reference to Captain Quon, who had not been privy to all of Kuda's missions, "that this will be your most dangerous mission. Your chances of living through it are impossible to predict. But, knowing you, my dear Konji, you will somehow manage."

Konji said, "After I am through with my makeup kit, I will look like a caucasian bridge worker. I have spent time in a museum in Mackinaw City studying their appearance. And, the more dangerous our task is, the more I will enjoy it. This one will require my greatest skills, both mentally and physically. But, I concentrate on the rewards if.... no, when we are successful, Chaw Wi."

Chaw Wi continued, "Now we must talk about the bomb. The Consortium of the countries that hate the United States most, provided the funds for Raja Putra to develop our small bomb. It is almost as powerful, in proportion to its size, as a nuclear bomb. So the miniature size bomb that is in your backpack is just strong enough to blow the Mackinac Bridge apart, and to kill thousands of people. We are only interested in killing those repugnant Republican candidates, but there will be five or ten thousand people on the bridge right behind them. We have no other choice."

"If these Republicans are elected, and they are favored to win, their platform will stamp out the drug trade. Our sponsors are not the drug peddlers themselves, but they know that alcohol and drug abuse are the most destructive forces in America. They want the drug trade to continue. It will eventually weaken and destroy the United States. That is their strategy..... they are very clever. They know they can't win a military war, so they will let immorality win it for them."

"Konji, you must develop your own plan to plant the bomb on the bridge at precisely thirty minutes before the Governor and his party reach the center. That is the most desirable time for the bomb to explode. After you set the bomb, you will have only thirty minutes to escape. The destruction caused by the bomb will not go beyond the five miles of the bridge itself. So as long as you get off the bridge, you will be safe. You can easily escape when the mass confusion begins. No one will pay attention to you, when there is absolute chaos everywhere."

Konji Kuda said, "I must have Tanaka with me. I need a decoy. He speaks little English, but looks caucasian. He is loyal, and will do whatever I ask. He will think the purpose of my mission is to inspect the Mackinac Bridge for a new Raja Putra product."

Captain Quon said, "I will tell him to prepare himself for travel with you."

Kuda said, "How much time do I have to meet you down near Algonac?"

Captain Quon said, "You will have at least ten hours. It will take you no more than six hours to drive there, so you have enough time to dispose of the car and board the ship. In the next two days you must select the exact spot where you will board, so we can be prepared to assist you if necessary."

Konji Kuda remained on the ship that Thursday night. The next day, when the three conspirators were satisfied that all of the details were covered, he and Tanaka left the *Kapitan Malaga*. They drove out of Chicago, onto Interstate

94, and headed toward a town neither one had ever heard of, Algonac, Michigan.

FRIDAY, AUGUST 30, 1996

The 31 Republican Governors met at the Mission Point Resort's convention room. Governor Broadwell was speaking.

"Tonight our dinner will be served right here in this room. I have invited Lake Superior State University Professor Clayton Hopping to be our after dinner speaker. Then tomorrow night, Senator Graham Fleming, the next President of the United States of America, will be our main speaker. The dinner and speech will be at the Grand Hotel. We'll have some news coverage tonight, but tomorrow they've promised me the works.... that is, major news coverage."

He flipped a couple of pages, "Now tomorrow morning, no meetings until after lunch, because I want you to enjoy Mackinac Island. Can you imagine.... a place in America with no cars racing all over the roads! Take your family for a coach ride, or rent bikes and ride around the Island.... it's only eight miles. You're back in the nineteenth century. Forget your phone and your television set. Force yourself to relax, and enjoy those magnificent horses. I know they usually say to stop and smell the roses, but here it's stop and smell the.... well.... maybe they don't say that here. I think it's stop and smell the lilacs."

There were a few scattered laughs, but the Governor's pun regarding the rather ubiquitous presence of horse manure went right over the heads of some.

FRIDAY NIGHT DINNER

After a delicious dinner of Michigan beef or Lake Trout, Michigan grown potatoes and asparagus, and for dessert, Traverse City cherry pie, Professor Clayton Hopping gave his speech.

"On May 5, 1994 the news had reported that an 18 year old American had received four swats with a cane, and a jail sentence of seven weeks. The number of swats and the length of the sentence were reduced by Singapore authorities yielding to political pressure from the President of the United States. Some Americans had objected to the young man's original punishment of six swats with a cane, calling it inhumane and unjustified for the magnitude of the crime."

"The only thing inhumane was that during the seven weeks that the young man was safe in jail, more than 1,000 young Americans died violently in the United States because of alcohol-related accidents, and another 1,000 or more died in drug-related violence. Our no swat policy, the complete absence of discipline, in the United States encourages teenagers and college students to drink alcohol excessively, or to take drugs. In this stupor they are more likely to commit crimes, ruining their lives as well as the lives of the victims."

"Crime in America is going to get worse in the next decade. There will be tens of thousands more teenage criminals, who are most likely to commit murders, rapes, and robberies. And these are the criminals who randomly rob and murder innocent strangers, with no remorse or emotion."

"The rewards for committing crimes are enormous. Besides the prospect of loot from the crime, there is the growing possibility of lawsuits and book contracts. When the guilty perpetrator of an unusually heinous crime is not convicted, due to a technicality, it means the possibility of a book contract, and becoming an instant millionaire. What a temptation! Our social and legal system has now made murder, especially the most heinous type, the easiest way to get rich quick, easier by far than winning the lottery!"

Dr. Hopping hesitated for a few seconds to let the audience absorb his pungent words, then continued.

"How can a society effectively stop 50 million Americans from smoking in public places, but fail completely to stop the killing caused by alcohol and drug abusers. Of course, teenagers will die from lung cancer if they smoke for an average of thirty to forty years, but more than 150 young Americans will die this week, and every week of the year from alcohol and drug abuse. Greedy radicals have already destroyed the lives of millions of teenagers who have suffered from alcohol and drug problems. Their tactics have been to completely emasculate the legal process to save the lives of a few worthless drug dealers who kill our children."

"These are my solutions to our major problems. First, we must have a foolproof law to stop the tricks that irresponsible lawyers use to free drug smugglers."

"And second, we have to get even tougher. We must officially declare war against drugs by an act of Congress. Enforce martial law against drug dealers. Anyone pursued in the act of bringing drugs into the country would be treated as if they were enemy soldiers. All dealers captured by the military would receive the death penalty. The trial and execution would be carried out by the military, under wartime rules. This is the only realistic way to substantially stop illegal drugs from entering the United States."

"When it comes to immorality, there is no easy solution. How does a nation restore family values? The leaders in our society, especially the parents, must radically challenge the popularity of immorality promoted by the entertainment world. But the traditional family of the past is rapidly disappearing, which means less parental influence."

"Rock stars, movie actors, and sports figures have more influence on some young people than parents do. These heroes are the Not-for-Profit Prostitutes, both men and women, and sexual promiscuity is their main activity, in movies, on the television screen, and on the college campuses. The unregulated teenager will be exposed to more than 3,000 scenes of adultery, or fornication on the television screen in one year."

The response to Professor Hopping's speech was mixed. Some conservatives thought it was too bland, and moderates were cautious. Several governors commented that there were too many legal considerations.... or it would be hard to convince enough congressmen. Or we can't move too fast or we'll lose the younger voters. The majority of the governors favored the idea of a stronger platform against crime.

CHAPTER 22

S am Green met Senator Graham Fleming at the Chippewa County Airport. Three limousines were awaiting his entourage. They followed Sam to St. Ignace where they boarded a special Star Lines ferry to Mackinac Island. At the Island the Senator insisted on walking to the Grand Hotel with Sam. Two bodyguards ambled, inconspicuously, if that is possible, several yards behind them.

"I'm not going to have much time, Sam. What has been happening since we last met? You told Governor Broadwell and me that you were looking into the bombing of that Singapore freighter.... and that some international plot to harm us, involving some Middle East countries, was possible."

Sam was ambivalent about telling the Senator the magnitude of his concern. He said, "Senator, your life is in danger.... if our suspicions are correct. We.... that includes Professor Kendall and members of the international anti-crime group I am working with.... think that these hate America countries would like to take you and Dan out of the picture. We believe that the Labor Day Bridge Walk is the most likely target."

The Senator stopped walking, and hesitated for a moment, as if shocked into seriousness.

Sam continued, "You said it yourself, Senator.... that you are proposing the first effective measure to stop drug trafficking.... and if you win the election it will put an end to the drug problem in America. That means an end to billions of dollars of drug money that is funnelled to foreign terrorists.... and they know it."

Walking briskly again, Senator Fleming said, "Can't the FBI and the CIA do something to stop them?"

"I considered asking for official FBI help from my superiors, but I have no proof or tangible evidence. It's more of a gut feeling.... based on the strange activities of an organized terrorist for-hire group. And you know very well what the news media did to the FBI in the Freemen standoff in Montana. The FBI had tangible, convincing, and incontrovertible evidence that laws were broken. But, the threat of a discrediting news attack, like that in Waco, was enough to compel them to back off and wait. Right now, in this country, law enforcement is in a no win situation. If I take serious measures and we're wrong.... I look like a fool....

and maybe even lose my job. And, if I don't, you could be dead, and I would be criticized.... and probably lose my job. But, I do have my own team that will be ready to act swiftly. And they're the ones who've been studying this terrorist group."

"Look Sam, you have it straight from me.... and I'll tell Governor Broadwell.... I'm sure he'll agree. We will keep this to ourselves, knowing that you and your team are watching out for us.... if there is a danger."

"One precaution you could take, Senator is to cancel the Bridge Walk. We think that is the greatest possibility of danger."

"Heavens, no. That is one of the highlights of our campaign. Nothing is more exhilarating to me than the Bridge Walk. I've been wanting to do it for a long time. I'm just not going to worry about it with you on the job."

Sam thought.... thanks a lot.... but didn't say it. When the long white porch of the Grand Hotel loomed ahead of them Sam knew that the Senator wanted to enjoy the splendor of this particular view of the Straits of Mackinac, unsurpassed by any other in the world.

That night the governors and key Republican party members had a royal banquet and Senator Fleming gave a highly persuasive speech, free from political rhetoric. In his entire campaign he chose not to bombast the incumbent Democratic President, but to state his convictions. Both the politicians and media were critical, but the general public welcomed the refreshing input of honesty and sincerity in a positive campaign. They were fed up with demeaning political cliches.

Sunday, September 1, 1996

Brad set up his telescope aimed at the Mackinac Bridge. Reino drove to the cottage from the Sault in the early afternoon. Alina rushed out to greet him. "Hello Captain Asuma.... I mean Reino. Have I been pronouncing it right? Is it Raye-no.... or Rye-no?

Reino said, "However you say it, Alina, is the best!"

Brad interjected, humorously irritated over Alina's attentiveness to his friend, "It's Raye-no if you want to sound like a Soumilainen.... that's what they call Finns."

The four friends sat on the porch overlooking the Straits. There were windows in all directions to offer a panoramic view of Lake Michigan, the Mackinac Bridge, St. Ignace, and Mackinac Island.

Brad began. "I will stay and watch on the telescope. Sam has provided two-way communication for all of us. He suggested that you be on the bridge, Reino, anywhere between the two towers. Billy will be in front of the Governor's party, which begins the walk at 7:30 in the morning."

A low groan was heard from Billy, "This is supposed to be my vacation..... you remember the words, Brad..... rest and relaxation."

"We'll be getting up very early, Billy. The school buses that take the walkers over to the St. Ignace side of the bridge begin at about six in the morning. Reino will get a ride on one of the buses, and hop off between the towers.... no.... on second thought you better stay at the South Tower, Reino. Sam has provided an orange vest, like the traffic directors who are stationed every few hundred yards along the bridge.

Remember, there are two lanes open for traffic, and two lanes for the walkers."

"Alina will be at this end of the bridge where the greeters stand is located. Ask for Stan, or whoever is in charge. The official greeter welcomes the celebrities as they come off the bridge. I remember in 1992, when everyone on the stand was waiting with anticipation to shake hands with President Bush. Just before he and Mrs. Bush reached the steps of the greeting stand, the Secret Service whisked them away to the school playground. Two huge helicopters swallowed them up and roared into the sky to the former Kincheloe Air Base, where Air Force One was waiting. What a disappointment that must have been for the greeters."

Then Brad said, "We'll take turns getting some sleep. Someone has to be on the telescope from now on. Right now, each of you has to memorize the fax from George. I've already done it. It shows the way to defuse the bomb. That plant manager of Bhari's said it would be almost impossible without knowing this system. The wires that are revealed to the bomb experts, or whatever they're called, are all fakes. There's a small compartment at the side, that has the real wires. I'll make a copy of the fax for each of you to study."

※

Konji Kuda and Tanaka stayed in a motel in Algonac on Friday and Saturday. Kuda drove all along the ship channels above Lake St. Clair, until he selected a perfect location for boarding the *Kapitan Malaga*. Then on Sunday the two men drove over to Frankenmuth, and had an abundant feast on the family style chicken dinner at the Bavarian Inn. They took their time driving up Interstate 75, arriving in Mackinaw City thirty minutes before six o'clock, as planned. The small motel that Chaw Wi had selected was west of the Mackinac Bridge, just three short blocks from the shore of the Straits. Kuda was instructed to pay the bill in advance so they could depart quickly the next morning.

Labor Day, September 2, 1996

Beginning very early on Monday morning, the school buses began driving over the Mackinac Bridge. They were moving slowly, bumper to bumper, as they carried full loads of eager bridge walkers. As was common in early September, the weather was cool, with the hint of a drizzle. The water was still warm from the summer heat, but the air was cool, causing a heavy mist or fog over the water. This morning it was thick for about thirty feet above the water surface. A bridge worker, obvious by the yellow iron worker's hat, and what looked like a tool kit strapped to his waist, stepped down from one of the buses at Pier 18. The workman nodded a thank you to the bus driver.

He climbed over the side of the iron railing and crawled out of sight. Pier 18, between the anchorage pier and the tower pier, is called the cable bent pier, where the two massive cables that hold the bridge up, bend downward into the anchorage pier. The distance between the two anchorage piers measures the true length of the suspension bridge.

These two enormous blocks of cement, reaching down into bedrock, support the entire system.

The workman climbed down into the truss span, the steel girders under the roadbed, and walked slowly and cautiously in the direction of Pier 19, the south tower pier. The distance between cable bent Pier 18 and south tower Pier 19 was 1,800 feet. The bus stopped momentarily at the south tower pier, to allow a second bridge worker to get off.

Brad was having a cup of coffee, as usual. At 7:00, and every five minutes, he stopped to take another glance through the telescope. He started at the St. Ignace side, where he could see the Governor's entourage gathering for the Bridge Walk to begin at 7:30. There was a police car and a television van in front of the procession. They would be at the center of the bridge at about 8 o'clock. Susan Young was on top of the van with a microphone in her hand.

At 7:15, Brad again moved the telescope slowly along the roadbed of the bridge from the St. Ignace end to the Mackinaw end. He saw a figure near the south cable bent pier moving in the direction of the south tower pier. He picked up the radio, and called Sam, on the Coast Guard Cutter Biscayne Bay.

"Sam, check if there should be a workman on the bridge right now. I have to know immediately."

Two minutes later Sam called back, "Brad I got through to Julie, the General Bridge Engineer. She said absolutely not."

"Thanks Sam. I'll get Reino."

"Reino, Reino, do you hear me?"

"Yes, Brad, I hear you."

"Where are you right now?"

"I'm at the south tower, Brad. That's where you wanted me, isn't it?"

"Yes, but there is someone posing as a workman climbing around by the south cable bent pier. It's Kuda, I'll bet."

Reino said, "I'll be there in a jiffy.... I've been waiting for this moment for a long time."

Brad said, "I'll monitor everything from here.... keep your radio on."

Reino raced on foot over to the cable bent pier. He crawled over the railing, and carefully climbed down one of the angled steel girders of the truss span under the road-bed. It was no easy task. The truss spans that supported the road were forty feet high. He reached the bottom outside girder, and began to walk carefully from span to span.

The horizontal outside girder was wide enough to walk on, about 30 inches. From that level it was about 150 feet straight down to the water. With no rails, it was not advisable to look down. Reino also had to stop at each V shaped intersection, and crawl around the vertically slanted girders.

The mysterious workman had moved, in the same manner, about halfway to the tower pier. Then, strangely.... he stopped and waited, as if to rest.

Reino eventually caught up with him. Waving his gun, so the man could see it, he shouted, "Stop.... who are you.... and what are you doing here?"

The man looked confused and didn't answer. He then

continued to proceed along the steel girders toward the tower. Reino finally caught up with him, and grabbed his shirt. The man turned abruptly and knocked the gun out of Reino's hand. Reino's right hand smashed him in the face. He frantically turned and ran. After a few steps he lost his balance and tumbled off the truss span. He fell 150 feet into the brisk waters of the Straits of Mackinac and disappeared.

Brad saw the body fall into the water through the telescope and said, "You got him Reino.... you got Kuda. Good work.... you finally stopped the monster."

Reino's radio was strapped to his chest so he heard Brad's voice. "I don't feel like a hero, Brad. He hardly put up a fight. I thought Kuda was strong as an ox. This guy was a pushover."

Brad said, "You're the ox, Reino. That's why it was so easy."

At the other end the news had just reached the Governor's party. A reporter stationed at the south end of the bridge saw the body fall from the bridge, and reported it to Susan.

She climbed down from the van and informed the Governor and Senator Fleming. "Do you want to stop the walk, Governor? There may be danger."

Governor Broadwell said, "A man fell off the Mackinac Bridge a few years back on Labor Day, but it didn't stop the walk. I have full confidence in our head of security. We won't stop unless he insists on it. Do you agree Graham?"

Senator Fleming replied, "Indeed I do, Dan. The poor

fellow.... his relatives, that is.... have our sympathy, but we must finish the walk."

Then Brad saw it. Another figure.... at the tower pier. It looked like another workman crawling in the girders below.

"Wait Reino, there's someone at the south tower pier."

Reino said, "I just came from there."

Brad informed him, "It looks as if you can walk on the truss span from where you are faster than going back to the cable bent pier and climbing back up to the roadway. Let's see.... you are only about 200 yards away. But, be careful.... go slow, so you don't fall, too."

"Okay, I'm on my way."

Brad called Sam on the *Biscayne Bay*, "Sam, do you hear me?"

"I hear you, Brad. What's up?"

"Trouble on the south tower pier. Get there as fast as you can. Reino is going after someone.... you know who.... right now."

Sam said, "Okay, but there's a damn fog over the water.... it's only twenty or thirty feet, but we can't see a thing on the surface. Hey, I thought the other guy was.... you know who."

Brad said, "There were two of them. Anyway.... just get as close as you can, and I'll let you know what I can see from here."

The *Biscayne Bay* moved closer to the south tower, having to be concerned with the ship channel, which went directly under the center of the bridge. They had received word that the 1,000 foot *Indiana Harbor* would be approaching the Mackinac Bridge from Lake Michigan in about forty-five minutes, and an upbound Greek ship, the *Pyrros*, was two hours away.

Brad watched as Reino walked along the wide outside girder of the struss span. He had to walk carefully between each section. One slip and he would plunge to the water below. A person could possibly survive the fall at this distance from the water, but it was unlikely. He started toward the tower at 7:30 a.m., about the time that the Bridge Walk was scheduled to begin.

Kuda had climbed to where the truss span joined with the cross span, or connecting section, between the two legs of the tower. There was more room for him to maneuver. He took the heavy backpack off, and used the straps to attach it to a bridge girder. Then he carefully set the triggering device for 8:15.

He turned around to leave, and looked into the face of Reino Asuma. Reino threw a fist at him. The blow bounced off Kuda's arm, which reflexively clamped around Reino's neck in a vice grip. Kuda executed his fatal twist that instantly extinguished his enemies. But Reino's powerful neck and arm muscles counteracted the thrust and broke his hold.

Kuda raged in humiliation. His leg thrust out catching Reino in the stomach. Reino fell backward off the platform. Fortunately, his body fell into the V section of the girders below. His head hit the metal, rendering him unconscious.

Kuda attached a long rope to a girder and rappelled

down the side of the tower pier into the fog. He disappeared from sight.

Brad frantically called, "Sam.... Sam."

"I hear you. Go ahead."

"Sam, he must be in the water.... Kuda or whoever it is. He disappeared into the fog. If he's alive he must be swimming around there somewhere. Try to find him. And Sam, we have to get Billy to the south tower pier.... and fast."

Sam said, "I know. We saw him coming down the tower, too. We're on the way, Brad. We'll get him."

Brad called, "Billy.... Billy, do you hear me?"

Billy responded quickly, "Yes Brad, I hear you."

"How fast can you get to the south tower pier?"

"It would take about twenty or thirty minutes for me to run three miles, or whatever it is. There are no cars here, except the bridge security police car that's leading the Bridge Walk."

Sam and Alina were both listening. Sam said, "I can order the driver to take you, Billy."

Alina practically shouted, "Wait.... I'm closer, and there's a police car right here by the welcome platform. There's no traffic on the walker's side of the bridge. I can get there in a few minutes."

Brad said, "No Alina, you're a.... I mean it's too dangerous."

"Alina replied, "Don't be silly, Brad. I studied the triggering device just like the rest of you."

Sam said, "She's right Brad. Alina.... go to the police car. I'll tell the driver to take you to the south tower. And

Billy, you get to the tower on foot as soon as you can.... but don't alarm the Governor's party."

Brad said, "Okay Sam. Now listen, Alina.... you know that Reino's been hurt. He hasn't moved for several minutes. When you get to the tower, climb over the side, and down to where Reino is. It's not easy. You have to climb down a slanted steel girder. You'll see when you get there. Hurry and I'll talk you along as you go."

Sam talked to Mackinaw City Police Chief, Ben Frayer, who was in the police car near the platform. He immediately agreed to drive Alina to the tower. She got off at the tower and proceeded to climb below. In the excitement she and Brad both forgot about her fear of heights. At the first step over the rail it dawned on her.

She kept her radio on, saying, "Oh, it's scary under here.... I can't look down.... I mustn't look down."

Brad said, "I know, I completely forgot about your.... but I'll keep talking, and you concentrate on that."

While Alina was climbing down, Reino woke up from his daze. It took a few seconds for him to recall why he was stretched out on a bridge girder, looking down 150 feet into the water. Then he carefully edged his way back to the cross span. He saw the bomb enclosure, and proceeded to open a front panel. Alina reached the cross span at that moment.

Alina called out, "Brad, are you there. Reino is okay. He's up and working on the bomb."

"Great.... I'm glad he's all right. Now, tell him to turn his radio on."

Reino reached down to locate his radio. It was gone.

"Tell Brad it must have fallen off. But it doesn't matter, Alina. We can both use your radio."

Reino was noticeably shaken up from his fall. His hands were trembling. Alina said, "Let me do it, Reino. You hold the radio while I work on the bomb."

Reino agreed and held the phone, while Alina said, "Brad, I assume this front panel is the fake, because it was the logical one to open up?"

"Right, Alina.... the right panel is on the left side. I mean.... the correct panel is on the left side. There is a finger sized hole. Poke it in and the panel will open. If it doesn't work, we're in trouble."

Alina found the hole and it worked. Inside were more wires. She had memorized the sequence.

"There is a timer here.... let's see.... it has fourteen minutes, and some rapidly moving seconds on it now. That gives us time to go over the sequence. I'll repeat it to you. You stop me only if I make an error."

Brad said, "Okay, go ahead. Make sure you have both the pliers and the wire cutter."

Alina said, "I do. First you detach with the pliers, not cut, the red wire. Within ten seconds you must cut the blue wire, and attach it to the red post. Second you cut the brown wire; then you have ten seconds to detach, not cut, the green wire from its post, and attach the brown wire to the green post."

Reino said, "Sounds like Danny Kaye in that old movie when we were kids, remember Brad.... now, what was the name of that movie?"

"Reino, you nut, forget the movie.... remember the bomb."

"Okay, okay, Alina's starting right now."

Alina carefully went through the sequence. She had to twist the cut wires onto the posts with the pliers so they wouldn't slip off.

A few minutes later Alina said, "Brad.... Reino....the timer stopped. I hope that's a good sign."

"How much time was left?" Brad asked.

Alina replied, "We still had six minutes.... plenty of time."

They all waited apprehensively until 8:15 a.m., when the bomb was set to explode. After ten more minutes, Reino sighed with relief, "I think we're safe now, Brad."

At the time the bomb was set to explode, Governor Broadwell and Senator Fleming had reached the south anchor pier. They were happily leading a stream of more than five thousand enthusiastic bridge walkers. Also at that time, the 1,000 foot self-unloading bulk carrier, *Indiana Harbor* was passing under the bridge, partly obscured by the fog.

Reino strapped the heavy backpack, with its now impotent message of doom, to his back. Sam's voice was heard on the radio, "Reino, Alina.... stay right there. The *Biscayne Bay* will get you off the tower from below."

"How are you going to do that? Reino wondered.

Sam said, "They'll shoot a line up to you, and you guide it around the girders. Then they'll attach a basket and bring you two down. I want that bomb down here in the *Biscayne Bay*."

Brad broke in, "Sam, did you find him?"

"No, sorry Brad. We have ships all over the area. But, no sign of Kuda, or his body."

Brad said, "Good work, everyone. See you back here at the cottage as soon as you can, Sam. I'll drive the car up to the gas station this side of the bridge. The town's too packed with cars to get any closer. I'll wait there to pick up Alina, Reino and Billy, and drive them back to the cottage."

CHAPTER 23

An exhausted man, assumed to be a hardy swimmer or a scuba diver, emerged from the water at the beach a few yards west of Fort Michilimackinac. He dragged himself up on shore at 7:55 a.m. There were few tourists on the west side of the bridge, and no one paid attention to the swimmer as he walked the short distance to his small motel. The large, muscular man quickly changed into dry clothes. He packed his belongings and hopped into his rented car. Then he drove on a road, carefully marked out on his map, that circled the town and avoided all the congested traffic.

By 8:10 a.m. he was driving south along Interstate 75. He periodically looked at his waterproof watch, and then in his rear view mirror. He stopped the car at exactly 8:14 a.m., three miles south of Mackinaw City, where you could still see the top of the Mackinac Bridge. He got out of the car and stared at the bridge, a smile of satisfaction on his face. At 8:16 a.m. his smile changed to a look of anger. He took his watch off, and smacked it against the side of the car. It kept on ticking. At 8:18 he looked at his watch again, scowled, got back into the car, and drove off. He turned his car radio on, trying to find a station with news. He mumbled what sounded like expletives in a foreign language, as station after station blasted his ears with a loud raucous noise, that he had heard some young Americans call music.

Fifty-five minutes later, he stopped at the Flap Jack Shack in Gaylord, Michigan for an enormous breakfast. Several hours later he arrived at Flint, and turned east on Interstate 69 to Port Huron. He then drove the short distance to Algonac.

Later that evening, the *Kapitan Malaga* passed through a narrow section of the ship channel near Harsen's Island. A man swam from the shore, out to the foreign freighter, and climbed up the Jacob's Ladder.

"Welcome aboard, Konji. We have a lot to discuss, but you must be cold and tired. We were certain that we would never see you again.... in this world, that is. When you are dry and rested we can talk about everything."

Kuda changed to dry clothes and fell asleep. By the time he awakened the *Kapitan Malaga* was already in the Welland Canal. After a generous meal Kuda went to the Captain's cabin.

Captain Quon spoke first, "We have had no news of an explosion. And Tanaka did not return with you. It is time to tell us what happened, Mr. Kuda?"

"Mr. Tanaka was a decoy, but I did not expect him to be killed. He would have surrendered. He did not speak or understand English well. I told him that if he were arrested, to say that he was paid to help in examining the Mackinac Bridge. I saw him fall. He was attempting to escape from an American, the same one I grappled with. He must have been a policeman."

Chaw Wi asked, "Do you think he could have survived the fall?"

"I doubt it. I crawled down the side of the tower more than 100 feet, down to the fog, before I would attempt to jump into the water. And even then the plunge into the water was shocking. It took all my strength to survive this mission."

Chaw Wi asked, "Did you escape without being noticed? There has been no news of an attempted bombing. I do not understand."

Visibly perturbed, Kuda said, "Nor I? The American who killed Tanaka attacked me right after I had set the timer. We struggled and I knocked him out. I had no time to kill him." Kuda would never admit that Reino was able to break his death hold.

"I managed to swim to shore, and walk to the motel. I drove out of town, stopping to look at the time that I had set the timer, exactly 8:15. But it did not explode. Something must have gone wrong with the bomb. I know that I set the triggering device correctly. You and I practiced it to perfection, Chaw Wi. And even if the American threw it in the water, we know that it would still activate, and blow the foundation of the bridge out, collapsing the entire structure."

Chaw Wi said, "Then we do not know what happened. Or you are just making excuses for your failure to carry out the mission. So, my dear friend, Konji, why don't I blame you for this failure, and take a gun to your head while you sleep? Why am I not despondent over our enormous failure?"

Kuda said, "Knowing you, my dear friend, Chaw Wi, you have a good reason.... or you may fear that my evil spirit would return and stick wooden slivers up your fingernails."

"The reason I am not despondent is that we have not, and will not lose our two million dollar reward. Our sponsors do not know, or care, how we will eliminate their enemies. They have given us until the presidential election to accomplish our mission. They will never know that we failed this time, unless it appears in the news. And for some reason, which we cannot surmise, it did not."

Captain Quon queried, "But, Mr. Chan, won't the sponsors wonder what happened to the bomb?"

Chaw Wi answered, "There is one more bomb hidden in the Raja Putra warehouse. It cost our sponsors, the Anti-American Consortium, 50 million in U.S. dollars for the research to develop the two miniature bombs, each with the explosive power of a small nuclear bomb."

"I asked them for the first two bombs, Captain, to test

the triggering device of Mr. Bhari's company. Bhari himself trained me, and I trained Mr. Kuda, how to attach the triggering device to the bomb. I didn't guarantee the Consortium that we would use it for this mission. They merely required that we accomplish the objective of killing the two candidates. If we do, they won't care what happened to the other bomb. We will tell them that we needed both of them. Then we will receive the other two million U.S. dollars. And that is why, Konji, I am not unhappy."

"I see.... I am happy too, even though I risked my life for nothing. It will not happen again. Next time we use the bomb, we will be certain of success," said Kuda.

〜〜
〜〜

The Coast Guard dropped Sam, Alina, and Reino off at the docks. They walked to Brad's car at the gas station. Billy was already there. They all went to the cottage.

Sam began, "First, I want to say to all of you, especially Reino and Alina.... you saved the day. No one can imagine what horror would have resulted from that bomb."

Alina said, "And strangely enough, we're the only ones who will ever know what happened. Except.... are you going to tell the Governor and the Senator, Sam?"

"Yes, I want to tell them that there was a plot to kill them, so they'll take this thing seriously."

Reino asked, "Did the Coast Guard find any bodies yet?

"No, they will keep on looking."

"What happened to the bomb?" Billy asked.

"The bomb is on the *Biscayne Bay*. They will take it to the FBI Lear Jet at Kincheloe.... or Chippewa County Airport. Then I am flying to Honolulu for a meeting with George. I wonder if you two, Billy and Alina, would like to fly back home with me. When do you plan on going back to Hawaii?"

Alina said, "Our tickets are for Thursday."

Sam said, "Well, I want to leave very soon. Either Wednesday or Thursday. Would you like to cancel your flights and come with me."

Brad said, "I'd like to go too. May I fly with you, Sam?"

Sam said, "Definitely Brad. You're welcome to come. This is official business. Otherwise I wouldn't ask you to fly with me. This case isn't closed as long as any of those terrorists are still alive."

This was a shock to Alina. She smiled as she asked, "Don't you have to teach at Lake Superior State University in the Sault, Brad?"

"No, I start in January. I'm on a research leave this Fall. I need to do research on hula dancers in Honolulu."

Before the last statement had time to take effect, Brad said, "Just kidding! I'll be lecturing at Hawaii Pacific, U of H at Manoa and Hilo, and at Chaminade on my new book on activity-based costing."

Billy blurted out, "What are you talking about, Brad? Why didn't you tell us?"

"I wanted to surprise you both. I'll be there for three months."

When Sam and Reino were about to depart, Alina took

Reino's hands gently in hers and said, "It has been a great pleasure to know such a gentleman, Reino.... and such a hero. I'll never forget you."

Reino's pulse shot up, but he had to be satisfied with, "Thank you Alina. You are a beautiful person. And you're the one who saved the day. I let that Kuda guy get the best of me. I have to admit.... he is mighty strong.... or should I say was. I sure hope he didn't get away."

Then Reino whacked Brad on the arm, looked at Alina and quipped, "You're much too good for this guy, Alina."

THURSDAY, SEPTEMBER 5, 1996

Sam's Lear Jet landed at the Honolulu Airport at 4:35 in the afternoon. Billy had left his Mercedes 190E at the airport.

Sam took Billy's phone number and said, "I'll keep in touch with you. I have an appointment with George tomorrow." He then disappeared into Honolulu, while the trio drove to Billy's house in Waimanalo.

Before they left Mackinaw City, Brad had time to pack and close up the cottage for the three months. Billy insisted that Brad stay with him instead of finding an apartment. Alina would rather he had his own place, if only to have Brad to herself once in a while. This way her well meaning, but pain in the neck, brother would always be around.

The three of them went out to dinner a few times, but Brad did not make any attempt to be alone with her. He still seemed rather timid in the company of the beautiful Alina.

TWO WEEKS LATER

The *Kapitan Malaga* had passed through the Panama Canal, and was 500 miles south of Hawaii. An American aircraft carrier was cruising approximately 100 miles north of the foreign ship. On Thursday, September 19th, a Navy helicopter, carrying two men, left the aircraft carrier and flew in the direction of the foreign ship.

It was a beautiful, clear day on the ocean. The blue-green waves were calm. On the bridge of the *Kapitan Malaga*, Chaw Wi Chan asked Captain Quon, "When will we arrive in Singapore, Captain?"

"It will be six more days, Mr. Chan."

Chaw Wi said, "That gives us time to plan our next operation, Konji."

Kuda said, "I know what I must do first. The professor must be eliminated. Then I must deal with his Hawaiian friends. I believe they are brother and sister."

Kuda did not say it out loud, but he was more determined to get revenge on the policeman who had humiliated him on the Mackinac Bridge. Few of his adversaries had survived his death hold.

Chaw Wi said, "You will have no more than three weeks to carry out your plans. Then you and I will formulate our final plans to...."

Captain Quon interrupted, "Listen, what is that?"

Kuda said, "It sounds like a helicopter."

A seaman entered the bridge and reported, "Captain, Sir. An American helicopter is circling our ship. They have not sent a message."

Kuda yelled, "Shoot it down, Captain."

Captain Quon said, "No, you fool. We did nothing wrong. They are probably looking for a reported drug shipment. Just keep calm and they will fly away in a few minutes. It troubles me, however, that there was no communication from them. That is unusual..... very unusual, indeed."

Captain Quon ordered his radio operator to contact the helicopter, but there was no response. The helicopter hovered closely overhead for three more minutes, then as quickly as it came, it flew off and disappeared over the horizon.

〰〰

A few minutes later an explosion was recorded by Hawaiian, and other Pacific Ocean seismology stations. It was reported as equal to a small nuclear bomb. Investigations revealed that no country was involved in nuclear testing in the Pacific.

Billy and Brad were watching the news on a Honolulu television station when the explosion was reported. Two days later the news reported from Hong Kong that a ship registered in Hong Kong, the *Kapitan Malaga*, had failed to arrive in port as scheduled. It had apparently disappeared. Communications with the ship ended abruptly on September 19th.

MONDAY, SEPTEMBER 23, 1996

Billy's phone rang at three o'clock on Monday afternoon.

"Hello, Billy. It's Sam Green. Is Brad still there? I want to see both of you.... and Alina too, whenever it's convenient."

Billy said, "Today is fine. Where are you now?"

Sam said, "I'm staying at the Royal Hawaiian."

Billy gave him directions to his house in Waimanalo. "It'll probably take you forty minutes or so to get here."

Sam arrived in about forty minutes and greeted the two friends. He began, "Did you hear the news?"

Brad said, "Obviously you mean about the *Kapitan Malaga*. Yes we did."

"When I left you, two weeks or so ago, I had a meeting with George at Wo Fat's. He and I developed a plan. We went to the Pacific Region Naval Commander, who cooperates with George in his anti-crime efforts, whenever he is legally able to."

"First we unofficially told him what had happened, and of the continuing threat to national security from these terrorists. We all agreed how terrible it is in situations like this. Our solution was to request, officially, for permission to defuse a bomb that had been placed on the *Kapitan Malaga*. We explained that we were the only ones who had the formula to disable the triggering device. Some of this, as you three know, was really true."

"George and I both know how to fly a helicopter, so the

Commander ordered the aircraft carrier to take us within 100 miles of the foreign ship, and to let us use a Navy helicopter to go on our mission of mercy. I explained to anyone on the ship, who asked, that the heavy black backpack contained the tools to defuse the bomb."

"George and I flew out to the *Kapitan Malaga*. George circled while I set the timer on the bomb for twelve minutes. Then we dropped it into the smokestack, and hightailed it. After we were a good fifteen miles away, we turned to observe the explosion. The *Kapitan Malaga* just blew apart and literally disappeared. We couldn't see a thing after the explosion. It even rocked the helicopter it was so powerful."

"When we returned to the aircraft carrier, we explained that the bomb went off a few minutes before we arrived. So we had to turn around and come back to the carrier. If anyone had asked about the black bag, we were going to say that the blast jarred the door open, and it fell out. But no one asked."

〰〰

At six o'clock Billy said, "Alina is working tonight and wants us all to meet her at the Halekulani Hotel. You can tell her what happened to Chaw Wi and his gang when we see her there, Sam. She'll be happy to know that her life is no longer in danger."

Then Billy proudly announced, "She is the Manager of Customer Relations.... you know. She has reserved a table for all of us in the famous La Mer dining room at seven o'clock. George will meet us in the lobby at six forty-five."

Sam, Brad, and Billy, joined by George, were met in the spectacular lobby of the Halekulani Hotel by Alina, who was dressed in a beautiful aqua colored, flowered muumuu, with as orchid lei around her neck. The table was situated so that they looked across Waikiki Beach, to what has to be one of the most satisfying sights in Hawaii, the profile of Diamondhead.

After dinner, George made a little speech, "We all know that the threat of international terrorism will not stop because of this one success, but we must keep on trying. The world will never know what happened. They will never know what you and your friends in Michigan have done for them. But, that is the way the Information Network System operates.... in complete secrecy. And that is the very reason that we are so successful. Receiving credit, or more likely criticism, from the news media would destroy all our efforts to stop crime in the world. Anyone else would want the glory. They would write a book.... perhaps a movie. That would become their motive..... not stopping the vicious criminals in our society."

George went on, "You are the real heroes.... and no one will ever know it! I'm proud of you..... even Sam here. I know that he is paid to do this, but he did a magnificent job of cooperating with us."

∼∼∼

Two days later, Sam returned to Detroit. Brad phoned Reino and explained what had occurred. Reino was not to tell Susan any details, but he took her out to dinner to celebrate their new, more serious relationship.

That same night Brad, Billy, and Alina went out to dinner at the Yum Yum Tree in Kailua. After dinner, Billy said, "Brad, I have some work to do tonight. Would you drop me off at the house first, and then drive Alina home in my car."

"Sure Billy, I'd be glad to."

Alina sparkled at the suggestion. When Brad walked her to the door, she gave him the traditional Hawaiian kiss on each cheek. Then to her surprise, Professor Bradley Kendall..... completely out of character..... put his arms around her, pulled her up tight, and gave her a long, soft kiss on the lips. Shocked with such aggressive behavior.... for him, that is.... but in celebration of her final victory over his timidity.... she responded passionately.

After the unexpected kiss, Alina looked up at Brad, with her twinkling brown eyes and captivating smile dazzling him, and coyly said, "Goodnight, Professor Kendall."

Brad, whose shell of academic objectivity had been cracked open by this explosion of genuine love, fumbled the words, "No, it's Brad, Alina..... call me Brad.... darn it.... tomorrow. I'll call you tomorrow. We'll go to dinner. I want to tell you how much.... " He hesitated, "We'll go to the Black Orchid.... without Billy.... just the two of us.... tomorrow."

Alina stalled just three seconds to increase the tension, and said, with a mischievous, but unmistakable air of Scarlet in her classic reply, "I'll think about that.... Bradley.... tomorrow!"

About the Author

Ronald J. Lewis resides in Mackinaw City, Michigan with his wife, Margaret. They have three children, Jeffrey, Randall, and Gary.

In 1965, Lewis received a Ph.D. in accounting and finance from Michigan State University, and he became the first Acting Dean of the new School of Business at Northern Michigan University. In 1969, he became Dean of Business at Tri-State University in Indiana, and was appointed Vice-President of Academic Affairs at Tri-State in 1973.

During his academic career he wrote two accounting textbooks, and two post-graduate accounting books for his lectures in Singapore and Malaysia. He spent his last ten academic years at Central Michigan University.

Mr. Lewis was listed in *Outstanding Educators in America* in 1972, and in *Who's Who in the Midwest* in 1977, 1989, and 1991.

Not until his retirement in 1992, did Mr. Lewis begin writing mystery novels as a way to relax from the analytical rigor of accounting.

MURDER IN MACKINAC

BY

RONALD J. LEWIS

"It is a very long time since I've read a mystery novel with so stunning an opening, and what is good about this mystery, is that it fulfills that promise: it is fast moving and filled with new incidents throughout. The geographical and chronological axes are also unusually wide and well-researched: from Mackinaw to Hawaii and from WWII and Finland's history to the present day. Sense of place is wonderfully conveyed and the contrasts between the physical characteristics and differing life-styles of Mackinac and Oahu are portrayed with a wealth of convincing detail and local color. I loved this novel; it is gripping and compelling from page 1 to 238. I will certainly read it again."

Gordon Williams, Thacher Professor of Latin
Yale University

"If you're fed up with the trash running across the screen night after night, run don't walk to your nearest bookstore for a copy of Ronald Lewis' skillfully written, *Murder in Mackinac*. Mystery fans who prefer crime with a touch of class will enjoy intrigue and romance woven into a convincing and well-researched story line. This is a sturdy work from a new author who proves morality, ingenuity, and the landscapes of three cultures can mix up a marvelous mystery novel. From first page to the surprising conclusion, you'll soon be an enthusiastic fan. Put out the *Do not Disturb* sign and spend a delicious evening of reading all the way along."

Suzanne Sawyer, Field Editor
Michigan Wilderness Journal

Additional Information

If you are unable to obtain a copy of either *Terror at the Soo Locks* or *Murder in Mackinac,* or if you would like to contact the author or publisher, please use the following address:

Ronald J. Lewis
c/o Agawa Press
P.O. Box 39
Mackinaw City, Michigan 49701
616/436-7032